FIVE ON FINNISTON FARM

Five On
Finniston Farm

Enid Blyton

*Hodder
Children's
Books*

a division of Hodder Headline Limited

First published in Great Britain in 1960
by Hodder and Stoughton

This edition 1991

For further information on Enid Blyton, please contact
www.blyton.com

20 19 18 17

A Catalogue record for this book is available from the
British Library.

ISBN 0-340-54892-4

Printed and bound in Great Britain by
Clays Ltd, St Ives plc

Hodder Children's Books
A Division of Hodder Headline Ltd
338 Euston Road
London NW1 3BH

Contents

1 The Five are all together again

'Phew!' said Julian, mopping his wet forehead. 'What a day! Let's go and live at the equator – it would be cool compared to this!'

He stood leaning on his bicycle, out of breath with a long steep ride up a hill. Dick grinned at him. 'You're out of training, Ju!' he said. 'Let's sit down for a bit and look at the view. We're pretty high up!'

They leaned their bicycles against a nearby gate and sat down, their backs against the lower bars. Below them spread the Dorset countryside, shimmering in the heat of the day, the distance almost lost in a blue haze. A small breeze came wandering round, and Julian sighed in relief.

'I'd never have come on this biking trip if I'd guessed it was going to be as hot as this!' he said. 'Good thing Anne didn't come – she'd have given up the first day.'

'George wouldn't have minded,' said Dick. 'She's game enough for anything.'

'Good old Georgina,' said Julian, shutting his eyes. 'I'll be glad to see the girls again. Fun to be on our own of course – but things always seem to happen when the four of us are together.'

'*Five*, you mean,' said Dick, tipping his cap over his eyes. 'Don't forget old Timmy. What a dog! Never knew one that had such a wet lick as Tim. I say – won't it be fun to meet them all! Don't let's forget the time, Julian. Hey, wake up, stupid! If we go to sleep now we won't be in time to meet the girls' bus.'

Julian was almost asleep. Dick looked at him and laughed. Then he looked at his watch, and did a little calculating. It was half past two.

'Let's see now – Anne and George will be on the bus that stops at Finniston Church at five past three,' he thought. 'Finniston is about a mile a way, down this hill. I'll give old Julian fifteen minutes to have a nap – and hope to goodness I don't fall asleep myself!'

He felt his own eyes closing after a minute, and got up at once to walk about. The two girls and Tim *must* be met, because they would have suitcases with them, which the boys planned to wheel along on their bicycles.

The Five were going to stay at a place called Finniston Farm, set on a hill above the little village of Finniston. None of them had been there before, nor even heard of it. It had all come about because George's mother had heard from an old school friend, who had told her that she was taking paying guests at her farmhouse – and had asked her to recommend visitors to her. George had promptly said she would like to go there with her cousins in the summer holidays.

'Hope it's a good place!' thought Dick, gazing down into the valley, where cornfields waved in the little breeze. 'Anyway, we shall only be there for two weeks – and it *will* be fun to be together again.'

He looked at his watch. 'Time to go!' He gave Julian a push. 'Hey – wake up!'

''Nother ten minutes,' muttered Julian, trying to turn over, as if he were in bed. He rolled against the gate-bars and fell on to the hard dry earth below. He sat up in surprise. 'Gosh – I thought I was in bed!' he said. 'I could have gone on sleeping for hours.'

'Well, it's time to go and meet that bus,' said Dick. 'I've had to walk about all the time you were a sleep, I was so afraid I'd go off myself. Come on Julian – we really must go!'

They rode down the hill, going cautiously round the sharp corners, remembering how many times they had met herds of cows, wide farm carts, tractors and the like, on their way through this great farming county. Ah – there was the village, at the bottom of the hill. It looked old and peaceful and half-asleep.

'Thank goodness it sells ginger beer and ice-creams!' said Dick, seeing a small shop with a big sign in the window. 'I feel as if I want to hang out my tongue, like Timmy does, I'm so thirsty!'

'Let's find the church and the bus stop,' said Julian. 'I 'I saw a spire as we rode down the hill, but it disappeared when we got near the bottom.'

'There's the bus!' said Dick, as he heard the noise of wheels rumbling along in the distance. 'Look, here it comes. We'll follow it.'

'There's Anne in it – and George, look!' shouted Julian. 'We're here exactly on time! Hey, George!'

The bus came to a stop by the old church, and out jumped Anne and George, each with a suitcase – and out leapt old Timmy too, his tongue hanging down, very glad to be out of the hot, jerky, smelly bus.

'There are the boys!' shouted George, and waved wildly as the bus went off again. 'Julian! Dick! I'm so glad you're here to meet us!'

The two boys rode up, and jumped off their bikes, while Timmy leapt round them, barking madly. They thumped the girls on their backs, and grinned at them. 'Just the same old couple!' said Dick. 'You've got a spot on your chin, George, and why on *earth* have you tied your hair into a ponytail, Anne?'

'You're not very polite, Dick,' said George, bumping him with her suitcase. 'I can't think why Anne and I looked forward so much to seeing you again. Here, take my suitcase – haven't you any manners?'

'Plenty,' said Dick, and grabbed the case. 'I just can't get over Anne's new hair-do. I don't like it, Anne – do you, Ju? Ponytail! A donkey tail would suit you better Anne!'

'It's all right – it's just because the back of my neck was so hot,' said Anne, shaking her hair free in a hurry. She hated her brothers to find fault with her. Julian gave her arm a squeeze.

'Nice to see you both,' he said. 'What about some ginger beer and ice-cream? There's a shop over there that sells them. And I've a sudden longing for nice juicy plums!'

'You haven't said a word to Timmy yet,' said George, half offended. 'He's been trotting round you and licking your hands – and he's so dreadfully hot and thirsty!'

'Shake paws, Tim,' said Dick, and Timmy politely put up his right paw. He shook hands with Julian too and then promptly went mad, careering about and almost knocking over a small boy on a bicycle.

'Come on, Tim – want an ice-cream?' said Dick, laying his hand on the big dog's head. 'Hark at him panting, George – I bet he wishes he could unzip his hairy coat and take it off! Don't you Tim?'

'Woof!' said Tim, and slapped his tail against Dick's legs.

They all trooped into the ice-cream shop. It was half dairy, half baker's. A small girl of about ten came to serve them.

'Mum's lying down,' she said. 'What can I get you? Ice-creams, I suppose? That's what everyone wants today.'

'You supposed right,' said Julian. 'A large one each, please – five in all – and four bottles of ginger pop as well.'

'*Five* ice-creams – do you want one for that dog, then?' said the girl in surprise, looking at Timmy.

'Woof,' he said at once.

'There you are,' said Dick, 'he said yes!'

Soon the Five were eating their cold ice-creams, Timmy licking his from a saucer. Before he had had many licks, the ice-cream slid from the saucer, and Timmy chased it all the way round the shop, as it slid away from his vigorous licks. The little girl watched him, fascinated.

'I must apologise for his manners,' said Julian, solemnly. 'He hasn't been very well brought up.' He at once had a glare from George, and grinned. He opened his bottle of ginger beer. 'Nice and cold,' he said. 'Here's a happy fortnight to us all!' He drank half the glass at top speed, and set it down with a great sigh.

'Well, blessings on the person who invented ice-cream, ginger pop and the rest!' he said. 'I'd rather invent things like that any day than rockets and bombs. Ha – I feel better now. What about you others? Do you feel like going to find the farm?'

'Whose farm?' asked the little girl, coming out from behind the counter to pick up Timmy's saucer. Timmy gave her a large, wet and loving lick as she bent down.

'Ooooh!' she said, pushing him away. 'He licked all down my face!'

'Probably thought you were an ice-cream,' said Dick, giving her his hanky to wipe her cheek. 'The farm we want is called Finniston Farm. Do you know it?'

'Oh *yes*,' said the little girl. 'You go down the village street, right to the end, and turn up the lane there – up to the right. The farmhouse is at the top of the lane. Are you staying with the Philpots?'

'Yes. Do you know them?' asked Julian, getting out some money to pay the bill.

'I know the twins there,' said the girl. 'The two Harries. At least, I don't know them *well* – nobody does. They're just wrapped up in each other, they never make any friends. You look out for their old great-grandad – *he's* a one he is! He once fought a mad bull and knocked it out! And his *voice* – you can hear it for miles! I was real scared of going near the farm when I was little. But Mrs Philpot, she's nice. You'll like her. The twins are very good to her – and to their dad, too – work like farm hands all the holidays. You won't know t'other from which, they're so alike!'

'Why did you call them the two Harries?' asked Anne, curiously.

'Oh, because they've both . . .' began the child, and then broke off as a plump woman came bustling into the shop.

'Janie – you go and see to the baby for me – I'll see to the shop now. Run along!'

Away went the small girl, scuttling through the door.

'Little gasbag she is!' said her mother. 'Anything more you want?'

'No thanks,' said Julian, getting up. 'We must go. We're to stay at Finniston Farm, so we may be seeing you again soon. We liked the ice-creams!'

'Oh – so you're going there, are you?' said the plump woman. 'I wonder how you'll get on with the

Harries! And keep out of Grandad's way – he's over eighty, but he can still give a mighty good thumping to anyone who crosses him!'

The Five went out into the hot sun again. Julian grinned round at the others. 'Well – shall we go and find the nice Mrs Philpot – the unfriendly Harries, whoever they might be – and the fearsome great-grandad? Sounds interesting, doesn't it?'

2 Finniston Farm

The four children, with Timmy trotting beside them, walked down the hot, dusty village street until they came to the end, and then saw the lane turning off to the right, just as the little girl had told them.

'Wait a minute,' said Anne, stopping at a curious little shop at the end of the village street. 'Look – here's an interesting shop – it sells antiques. Look at those old horse-brasses – I'd like to get one or two of those. And just see those lovely old prints!'

'Oh *no* – not now, Anne,' said Julian, with a groan. 'This awful craze of yours for second-hand shops has been going on too long! Horse-brasses! You've got stacks of them already! If you think we're going to go into that dark, smelly little shop and . . .'

'Oh, I'm not going in *now*,' said Anne, hurriedly. 'But it does look rather exciting. I'll come by myself sometime and browse round.' She glanced at the name on the shop front. 'William Finniston – how funny to have the same name as the village! I wonder if . . .'

'Oh come *on*,' said George impatiently, and Timmy tugged at her skirt. Anne gave one backward glance at the fascinating little shop window, and hurried after the others, making up her mind to slip down to the shop one day when she was alone.

They all went up the little winding lane, where red poppy-heads jigged about in the breeze, and after a while they came in sight of the farmhouse. It was a big one, three storeys high, with whitewashed walls, and the rather small windows belonging to the age in which it was built. Old-fashioned red and white roses rambled over the porch, and the old wooden door stood wide open.

The Five stood on the scrubbed stone entrance, looking into the dim hall. An old wooden chest stood there, and a carved chair. A rather threadbare rug lay on the stone floor, and a grandfather clock ticked slowly and loudly.

Somewhere a dog barked, and Timmy at once barked back. 'WOOF, WOOF!'

'Be quiet, Timmy,' said George sharply, afraid that a horde of farm dogs might come rushing out. She looked for a bell or a knocker, but couldn't see either. Then Dick spotted a beautiful wrought-iron handle hanging down from the roof of the porch. Could it be a bell?

He pulled it, and at once a bell jangled very loudly somewhere in the depths of the farmhouse, making them all jump. They stood in silence, waiting for someone to come. Then they heard footsteps and two children came up the hallway.

They were *exactly* alike! The most twinny twins I've ever seen, thought Anne, in amazement. Julian smiled his friendliest smile. 'Good afternoon – we're the Kirrins – I – er – I hope you're expecting us.'

The twins stared at him without a smile. They nodded together. 'Come this way,' they both said, and marched back down the hall. The four stared at one another in surprise.

'Why so stiff and haughty?' whispered Dick, putting on a face exactly like the twins.' Anne giggled. They all followed the twins, who were dressed exactly alike in navy jeans and navy shirts. They went right down the long hall, passed a stairway, round a dark corner, and into an enormous kitchen, which was obviously used as a sitting room as well.

'The Kirrins, Mother!' said the twins, together, and at once disappeared through another door, shoulder to shoulder. The children found themselves facing a pleasant-looking woman standing by a table, her hands white with flour. She smiled, and then gave a little laugh.

'Oh, my dears! I didn't expect you quite so soon! Do forgive my not being able to shake hands with you – but I was just making scones for your tea. I'm so pleased to see you. Did you have a good journey here?'

It was nice to hear her welcoming voice and see her wide smile. The Five warmed to her at once. Julian put down the suitcase he was carrying and looked round the room.

'What a lovely old place!' he said. 'You carry on with your scone-making, Mrs Philpot – we'll look after ourselves. Just tell us where to go. It's nice of you to have us.'

'I'm glad to,' said Mrs Philpot. 'I expect your aunt told you the farm's not doing too well, and she kindly said she'd send you here for two weeks. I've some other boarders too – an American and his son – so I'm pretty busy.'

'Well, you don't need to bother too much about *us*,' said Dick. 'In fact, we'll camp out under a haystack if you like – or in a barn. We're used to roughing it!'

'Well – that *might* be a help,' said Mrs Philpot, going on with her mixing. 'I've a bedroom that would do for the girls all right – but I'm afraid you boys would have to share one with the American boy – and – er – well, you mightn't like him.'

'Oh, I expect we'll get on all right,' said Julian. 'But my brother and I would certainly *prefer* to be by ourselves, Mrs Philpot. What about putting up camp beds or something in a barn? We'd love that!'

Anne looked at Mrs Philpot's kind, tired face, and felt suddenly sorry for her. How awful to *have* to have your home invaded by strangers, whether you liked them or not! She went over to her.

'You tell Georgina and me anything you'd like us to do to help,' she said. 'You know – making the beds and dusting and things like that. We're used to doing things at home, and . . .'

'I'm going to enjoy having *you*!' said Mrs Philpot, looking round at them all. 'And you won't need to help very much. The twins do a great deal – too much, I think, bless them – because they help on the farm too. Now, you go up the stairs to the very top of the house, and you'll see two bedrooms, one on each side of the landing – the left-hand one is yours, girls – the other is where the American boy is sleeping. And as for you two boys, you can slip out to the barn, and see if you'd like a couple of camp beds there. I'll get the twins to take you.'

The twins came back at this minute, and stood silently shoulder to shoulder, as alike as peas in a pod George looked at them.

'What's your name?' she said to one twin.

'Harry!' was the answer. She turned to the other. 'and what's yours?'

'Harry!'

'But surely you don't have the same name?' exclaimed George.

'Well, you see,' explained their mother, 'we called the boy Henry, and he became Harry, of course – and we called the girl Harriet, and *she* calls herself Harry for short – so they're known as the Harries.'

'I thought they were both *boys*!' said Dick in amazement. 'I wouldn't know which is which!'

'Well, they felt they *have* to be alike,' said Mrs Philpot, 'and as Harry can't have long hair like a girl Harriet has to have shorter hair to be like Harry! I very often don't know one from the other myself.'

Dick grinned. 'Funny how some girls want to be boys!' he said, with a sly glance at George, who gave him a furious look.

'Twins, show the Kirrins up to the top bedroom,' said Mrs Philpot, 'and then take the boys out to the big barn. They can have the old camp beds, if they like the look of the barn.'

'*We* sleep out there,' said the Harries, both together, and scowled just like George.

'Well, you shouldn't,' said their mother. 'I told you to take your mattresses to the little room off the dairy.'

'It's too stuffy,' said the twins.

'Hang on – we don't want to cause trouble,' said Julian, feeling that the twins were too unfriendly for words. 'Can't *we* sleep in the room off the dairy?'

'Certainly not,' said Mrs Philpot, and sent the Harries a warning glance. 'There's room for you all in the big barn. Go on now, twins, do as I tell you, take the four up to the top bedroom, with the cases, and then out to the barn.'

The twins went to pick up the suitcases, still looking mutinous. Dick interposed himself between them and the cases. '*We'll* carry them,' he said stiffly. 'We don't want to be any more trouble to you than we can help.'

And he and Julian picked up a suitcase each, and set off after the Harries, who looked suddenly surprised. George followed with Timmy, more amused than

cross. Anne went to pick up a spoon that Mrs Philpot
had dropped.

'Thank you, dear,' said Mrs Philpot. 'Look – don't
get upset by the twins. They're a funny pair – but good
at heart. They just don't like strangers in their home,
that's all. Promise you won't mind them? I do want
you to be happy here.'

Anne looked at the kindly, tired face of the woman
beside her, and smiled. 'We'll promise not to worry
about the twins – if you'll promise not to worry about
us!' she said. 'We can look after ourselves, you know –
honestly, we're used to it. And please do tell us when
you want anything done!'

She went out of the room and up the stairs. The
others were already in one of the two bedrooms at the
top of the house. It was a fairly big room, whitewashed, with rather a small window and boarded
floors. Julian looked at the boards he was standing on.
'I say! Look at the wood this floor's made of – solid old
oak, worn white with the years! This farmhouse must
be very old. And look at the beams running across the
walls and into the roof. Hey, twins, this is a wonderful
old house!'

The twins unbent enough to nod in time together.
'Seems as if you two go by clockwork – you speak the
same words at the same time, you walk in time, you
nod your heads in time!' said Dick. 'But, I say – do you
ever smile?'

The twins looked at him with dislike. Anne nudged
Dick. 'Stop it, Dick! Don't tease them. Perhaps they'd
show you the barn now. We'll unpack some clean
things we've brought for you in our case, and come
down with them when we're ready.'

'Right,' said Dick, and he and Julian went out of the
room. Opposite, with its door open, was the other

room, where the American boy slept. It was so very untidy that Dick couldn't help exclaiming.

'Gosh – how does he get his room into all that mess?' He and Julian went down the stairs, and Dick turned back to see if the Harries were following. He saw them standing at the top, each shaking a furious fist at the door of the American boy's room. And what a furious look on their faces, too!

Whew! thought Dick. The Harries have got some sort of grudge against him – let's hope they don't get one for us, too. 'Well – now for the barn,' he said aloud. 'Don't go so fast, Ju. Wait for the twins – they're just falling over themselves to look after us!'

3 Out in the barn

The twins stalked out of the farmhouse and took the two boys round the dairy shed, and up to an enormous barn. One of them pushed open the great door.

'I *say*!' said Julian, gazing into the dark barn. 'I never saw such a great barn in all my life! It's as old as the hills – look at those beams soaring up into the roof – it reminds me of a cathedral, somehow. I wonder why they built the roof so high. What do you store in here, twins?'

'Sacks of meal,' said the Harries together, opening and shutting their mouths as one. The two boys saw a couple of camp beds in a corner of the barn.

'Look,' said Julian, 'if you really would rather sleep here alone, we'll sleep in the little room off the dairy that your mother spoke of.'

Before the twins could answer, a shrill barking came from the direction of the camp beds, and the boys saw a tiny black poodle there, standing up, quivering in every hair.

'What a tiny thing!' said Julian. 'Is he yours? What's his name?'

'Snippet,' came the answer from both at once. 'Come here, Snippet!'

At once the tiny black poodle hurled himself off the camp bed and raced over to them. He fawned on them all, barking in delight, licking everyone in turn. Dick picked him up, but the twins at once clutched Snippet themselves.

'He's OUR dog!' they said so fiercely that Dick backed away.

'All right, all right – you can have him. But be careful Tim doesn't eat him!' he said. A look of fear came over the faces of the Harries, and they turned to one another, anxiously.

'It's all right,' said Julian, hastily. 'Tim's gentle with small things. You needn't be afraid. I say – why do you have to be so *dumb*? It really wouldn't hurt you to be a bit friendly. And do let us sleep in your old room – we really don't mind.'

The twins looked at each other again, as if reading one another's thoughts, and then they turned gravely to the boys, not looking quite so unfriendly.

'We will *all* sleep here,' they said. 'We will fetch the other camp beds.' And off they marched, Snippet running excitedly at their heels.

Julian scratched his head. 'Those twins make me feel peculiar,' he said. 'I don't feel they are quite *real*. The way they act and speak together makes me feel as if they're puppets or something.'

'They're just jolly rude and unfriendly,' said Dick, bluntly. 'Oh well – they won't get in our way much. I vote we explore the farm tomorrow. It looks quite a big one – spreading out over the hill slopes everywhere. I wonder if we could get a ride on a tractor?'

At that moment a bell rang loudly from the direction of the house. 'What's that for?' said Dick. 'Tea, I hope!'

The twins came back at that moment with two more camp beds, which they proceeded to set up as far from their own as possible. Dick went to give a hand, but they waved him off, and put up the beds most efficiently and quickly by themselves.

'Tea is ready,' they said, standing up when the beds were finished, and blankets and pillows set out on them. 'We will show you where to wash.'

'Thanks,' said Dick and Julian together, and then grinned at one another. 'Better be careful,' said Julian, 'or we'll catch their habit of speaking exactly at the same moment. I say – isn't that poodle funny – look at him stalking that jackdaw!'

A black jackdaw, the nape of his neck showing grey as he ran in front of Snippet, had flown down from somewhere in the roof of the barn. As Snippet danced after him he ran behind sacks, scurried into corners and led the little dog such a dance that the two boys roared. Even the twins smiled.

'Chack!' said the jackdaw, and rose into the air. He settled himself on the middle of the poodle's back, and Snippet promptly went mad, and tore about the barn at top speed.

'Roll over, Snippet!' shouted the Harries, and Snippet at once flung himself on his back – but the jackdaw, with a triumphant 'chack' rose at once into the air, and alighted on one twin's head.

'I say, is he tame?' said Dick. 'What's his name?'

'Nosey. He's ours. He fell down a chimney and broke his wing,' said the twins. 'So we kept him till it was well and now he won't leave us.'

'Gosh!' said Dick, staring at them. 'Did you *really* say all that – or was it the jackdaw? You *can* talk properly, after all.'

Nosey pecked at the twin's ear nearest to him, and the twin gave a yell. 'Stop it, Nosey!' The jackdaw rose into the air, with a 'chack-chack-chack' that sounded very like a laugh, and disappeared somewhere in the roof.

Just then the two girls came to find the boys in the barn, sent by Mrs Philpot, who was sure they hadn't heard the bell. Timmy was with them, of course, sniffing into every corner, enjoying the farm smells everywhere. They came to the barn and looked in.

'Oh, there you are!' called Anne. 'Mrs Philpot said we . . .'

Timmy began to bark, and she stopped. He had caught sight of Snippet sniffing behind the sacks, still hunting for the cheeky jackdaw. He stood still and stared. What in the wide world was that funny little black creature? He gave another loud bark and shot over towards the poodle, who gave a terrified yelp and leapt into the arms of one of the twins.

'Take your dog away,' said both twins, fiercely, glaring at the four.

'It's all right – he won't hurt Snippet,' said George, advancing on Timmy and taking hold of his collar. 'He really won't.'

'TAKE YOUR DOG AWAY!' shouted the twins, and up in the roof somewhere the jackdaw said, 'CHACK, CHACK, CHACK!' just as fiercely.

'All right, all right,' said George, glaring as angrily as the twins. 'Come on, Tim. That poodle wouldn't be more than a mouthful for you, anyway!'

They all went back to the farmhouse in silence, Snippet having been left behind on the camp bed belonging to one of the twins. They cheered up when they came into the big, cool kitchen. Tea was now laid on the farmhouse table, a big solid affair of old, old oak. Chairs were set round and it all looked very home-like.

'Hot scones,' said George, lifting the lid of a dish. 'I never thought I'd like hot scones on a summer's day, but these look heavenly. Running with butter! Just how I like them!'

The four looked at the home-made buns and biscuits and the great fruit cake. They stared at the dishes of home-made jam, and the big plate of ripe plums. Then they looked at Mrs Philpot, sitting behind a very big teapot, pouring out cups of tea.

'You mustn't spoil us, Mrs Philpot,' said Julian, thinking that really his hostess was doing too much. 'Please don't let us make too much work for you!'

A loud, commanding voice suddenly made them all jump. Sitting in a big wooden armchair near the window was someone they hadn't seen – a burly old man with a shock of snowy white hair and a luxuriant white beard almost down to his waist. His eyes were startlingly bright as he looked across at them.

'TOO MUCH WORK! What's that you say? TOO MUCH WORK? Ha, people nowadays don't know what work is, they don't! Grumble, grumble, GRUMBLE, asking for this and expecting that! Pah! PAH, I say!'

'Now now, Grandad,' said Mrs Philpot, gently. 'You just sup your tea and rest. You've been out on the farm all day, and it's too much work for you.'

That set the old man off again. 'TOO MUCH WORK! Now let me tell you something. When I was a young lad, I . . . hallo, who's this?'

It was Timmy! He had been startled by the sudden shouting of the old man, and had stood up, his hackles rising, and a low growl down in his throat. And then a very curious thing happened.

Timmy walked slowly over to the fierce old man, stood by him – and laid his head gently on his knee! Everyone stared in astonishment, and George could hardly believe her eyes!

At first the old man took no notice. He just let

Timmy stay there, and went on with his shouting. 'No one knows anything these days. They don't know a good sheep or a good bull or a good dog. They . . .'

Timmy moved his head a little, and the old man stopped again. He looked down at Timmy, and patted him on the head. 'Now *here's* a dog – a REAL dog. A dog that could be the best friend any man ever had. Ah, he reminds me of my old True, he does.'

George was staring in amazement at Timmy. 'He's never done a thing like that before,' she said.

'All dogs are like that with old Grandad,' said Mrs Philpot softly. 'Don't mind his shouting. He's like that. See – your Timmy is lying down by Grandad – now they'll both be happy. Grandad will have his tea and be nice and quiet. Don't take any notice of him now.'

Still astonished, the children ate a marvellous tea, and were soon talking eagerly to Mrs Philpot, asking her questions about the farm.

'Yes, of course you can go on the tractor. And we've an old Land Rover too – you can motor round the farm in that, if you like. Wait till my husband comes in – he'll tell you what you can do.'

Nobody saw a little black shadow come in at the door, and sidle softly over to Grandad – Snippet the poodle! He had left the barn and come to the kitchen he loved. It was only when Mrs Philpot turned round to ask the old man to have another cup of tea that she saw a very strange sight indeed. She nudged the twins, and they hurried to look.

They saw Timmy lying peacefully down on Grandad's big feet – and Snippet the poodle lying between Timmy's great front paws! Well – what an astonishing sight to be sure!

'Grandad's happy now,' said Mrs Philpot. 'Two

dogs at his feet. And now, look – here's my husband! Come along in, Trevor – we're all here, the dogs as well!'

4 *Junior!*

A big man came into the kitchen, very like the twins to look at. He stooped, and seemed tired. He didn't smile, but just nodded.

'Trevor, here are the visitors I told you about,' said Mrs Philpot. 'Look, this is Julian and . . .'

'More visitors?' said Trevor with a groan. 'Good heavens – what a crowd of children! Where's that American boy? I've got a bone to pick with him. He tried to set the tractor going by himself this morning, and . . .'

'Oh, Trevor – never mind about that now. Just wash and come and have your tea,' said Mrs Philpot. 'I've kept some of your favourite scones for you.'

'Don't want any tea,' said her husband. 'Can't stop – except for just one cup, and that I'll take in the dairy. I've got to go and see to the milking. Bob's off today.'

'We'll help, Dad!' said the twins speaking together, as usual, and they got up from the table at once.

'No – you sit down,' said their mother. 'You've been on the go from seven o'clock this morning. Sit down and finish your tea in peace.'

'I could do with your help, twins,' said their father, as he went through the door towards the dairy, 'but now your mother's got so many on her hands, she'll need you more than I do!'

'Mrs Philpot – let the twins go if they want to,' said Julian at once. 'We can help, you know – we're used to helping at home.'

'And what's more, we like it,' said Anne. 'Do let us, Mrs Philpot – we'll feel much more at home then. Can't we clear away and wash up and all that, while the twins go and help with the milking?'

'YOU LET 'EM HELP!' shouted old Great-Grandad suddenly from his corner, making Timmy and Snippet leap to their feet, startled. 'WHAT ARE CHILDREN COMING TO NOWADAYS WAITED ON HAND AND FOOT? PAH!'

'Now, now, Grandad,' said poor Mrs Philpot. 'Don't you start worrying. We can manage fine.'

The old man made a loud, explosive noise, and banged his hand down on the arm of his chair. 'WHAT I SAY IS THIS . . .'

But he got no further, for the sound of footsteps could be heard in the hall, coming towards the kitchen, and loud, American voices came nearer and nearer.

'See here, Pop – I wanna come with you! This place is dead. You take me up to London with you, aw, Pop, go on, do!'

'That the Americans?' asked Dick, turning to the twins. Their faces had gone as black as thunder. They nodded. In came a burly man, looking rather odd in smart town clothes, and a fat pasty-faced boy of about eleven. The father stood at the door and looked round rubbing his hands.

'Hiya, folks! We've been over to that swell old town and picked up some fine souvenirs – my, my, they were cheap as dirt! We late for tea? Hallo, who're all these folks?'

He grinned round at Julian and the others. Julian

stood up politely. 'We're four cousins,' he said. 'We've come to stay here.'

'Stay here? Where you gonna sleep, then?' demanded the boy, pulling up a chair to the table. 'This is a one-eyed place, ain't it, Pop.'

'Shut up,' said the twins together, and gave the boy such a glare that Anne stared in astonishment.

'Aw, go on, I can say what I like, can't I?' said the boy. 'Free country, isn't it? Gee, you should just see America! That's something! Mrs Philpot, I'll have a bit of that cake – looks good to me.'

'CAN'T YOU SAY PLEASE?' roared a voice from the corner. That was Great-Grandad of course! But the boy took no notice, and merely held out his plate, while Mrs Philpot cut him an enormous slice of cake.

'I'll have the same as Junior, Mrs Philpot ma'am,' said the American, and sat down at the table. He held out his plate too. 'Say, you should see the things we've bought. We've had a day, haven't we, Junior?'

'Sure, Pop,' said Junior. 'Say, can't I have an iced drink? Look here – who's going to drink hot tea on a day like this!'

'I'll get you some iced lemonade,' said Mrs Philpot, rising.

'LET HIM GET IT HIMSELF! LITTLE BRAT!' That was Great-Grandad again, of course. But the twins were already up and on their way to fetch the orangeade themselves. George caught sight of their faces as they passed her, and had a shock of surprise. Goodness – how those twins hated that boy!

'That old grand-daddy of yours must be a bit of a nuisance to you,' said the American in a low voice to Mrs Philpot. 'Always butting in, isn't he? Rude old fellow, too.'

'NOW DON'T YOU SIT THERE WHISPERING!' shouted Grandad. 'I CAN HEAR EVERY WORD!'

'Now, now, Grandad, don't upset yourself,' said poor Mrs Philpot. 'You just sit there and have a nap.'

'No. I'm going out again,' said Great-Grandad heaving himself up. 'There's some people here that fair make me ill!'

And out he went leaning on his stick, a magnificent figure with his head of snow-white hair and his long beard.

'Like someone out of the Old Testament,' said Anne to Dick. Timmy got up and followed the old man to the door, with Snippet close behind him. Junior saw Timmy at once.

'Hey! Look at that big dog!' he said. 'Who's he? I've not seen him before. Hey, you, come and have a bun.'

Timmy took not the slightest notice. George addressed Junior in an icy voice. 'That's my dog Timmy. I don't allow anyone to feed him except me.'

'Shucks!' said Junior and threw the cake down on the floor, so that it slid to Tim's feet. 'That's for you dog!'

Timmy looked down at the cake, and stood perfectly still. Then he looked at George. 'Come here, Timmy,' said George, and he walked straight to her. The cake lay on the floor half-broken into crumbs.

'My dog is not going to eat that,' said George. 'Better pick it up, hadn't you? It's made a bit of a mess on the floor.'

'Pick it up yourself,' said Junior, helping himself to another bun. 'Gee – what a glare you've got! Makes me want my sunglasses, brother!' He gave George a sudden sharp dig in the ribs, and she gasped. Timmy was beside her in a moment, growling so deeply that Junior slid out of his seat in alarm.

'Say, Pop – this dog's fierce!' he said. 'He tried to bite me!'

'He did not,' said George. 'But he *might* bite if you don't do what I said, and pick up that bun!'

'Now, now,' said Mrs Philpot, really distressed. 'Leave it – it can be swept up afterwards. Will you have another piece of cake, Mr Henning?'

It really was an embarrassing meal, and Anne longed for it to be over. Junior quietened down considerably when he saw Timmy lying down between his chair and George's, but his father made up for that by talking non-stop about the 'wunnerful' things he had bought that day. Everyone was extremely bored. The twins came back with a jug of orangeade, which they placed on the table, with two glasses, in case Mr Henning wanted some. They then disappeared.

'Where have they gone?' demanded Junior, having poured a glass of orangeade straight down his throat in a most remarkable manner. 'Gee, that was good.'

'The twins have gone to help with the milking, I expect,' said Mrs Philpot, looking suddenly very weary. Julian looked at her. She must find these meals very tiring, he thought, coping with so many people. Junior piped up at once.

'I'll go and help with the milking,' he said, and slid off his chair.

'I'd rather you didn't, Junior,' said Mrs Philpot. 'You upset the cows a bit last time, you know.'

'Aw gee – that was because I was new to it,' said Junior. Julian looked at Mr Henning, expecting him to forbid Junior to go, but he said nothing. He lit a cigarette and threw the match down on·the floor.

George scowled when she saw Junior heading for the door. How dare he go out to the milking against the wishes of his hostess? She murmured a few words to Timmy, and he got up at once and ran to the door, barring it against Junior.

'Get out of my way, you,' said Junior, stopping. Timmy growled. 'Say, call him back, will you?' said Junior, turning round. No one said anything. Mrs Philpot rose and began to gather things together. It seemed to George as if she had tears in her eyes. No wonder, if this kind of thing happened every day!

As Timmy stood like a statue in the doorway, giving small threatening growls every now and again, Junior decided to give up. He dearly longed to give the dog a kick, but didn't dare to. He walked back to his father.

'Say, Pop – coming for a walk?' he said. 'Let's get out of here.'

Without a word father and son walked out of the other door. Everyone heaved a sigh of relief.

'You go and sit down and have a rest, Mrs Philpot,' said Anne. 'We'll do the washing-up. We'd love to!'

'Well – it's really kind of you,' said Mrs Philpot. 'I've been on the go all day, and twenty minutes' rest will do me good. I'm afraid Junior gets on my nerves. I do *hope* Timmy won't bite him!'

'He'll give him a nip before long,' said George cheerfully, collecting cups and saucers with Anne. 'What are you boys going to do? Go to the milking shed?'

'Yes. We've milked cows plenty of time,' said Dick. 'Nice job! I like the smell of cows. See you later, girls – and if that little pest tries any tricks, just give us a call! I'd love to rub his face into that crumby mess on the floor!'

'I'm just going to sweep it up,' said Anne. 'See you at supper-time!'

The boys went out, whistling. Mrs Philpot had

disappeared. Only George, Anne and Timmy were left, for Snippet had gone out with the Harries.

'I rather wish we hadn't come,' said George, carrying out a tray to the scullery. 'It's an AWFUL lot for Mrs Philpot to do. Still – if she needs the money . . .'

'Oh well – we can help – and we'll be out most of the day,' said Anne. 'We shan't see much of Junior – little beast!'

You're wrong, Anne. You'll see far too much of him! It's a good thing Timmy's there – he's the only one that can manage people like Junior!

5 Evening at the farm

George and Anne went out to find the others in the milking shed. There were plenty of cows there, swishing their tails. The milking was almost finished, and the twins were driving some of the cows back to the field.

'Hallo – how did you get on?' asked Anne.

'Fine – it was fun,' said Dick. 'My cows did better than Julian's, though – I sang to them all the time, and they loved it!'

'Silly!' said George. 'Did you have a talk with the farmer?'

'Yes – he says he's got an old Land Rover and he'll take us all over the farm tomorrow,' said Dick, pleased. '*And* we can ride on that tractor, if Bill – that's one of his farm hands – will let us. He says Bill won't have Junior on the tractor at any price – so maybe there'll be a row if he sees us on it!'

'Well, I'm all ready for a row, and so is Timmy,' said George grimly. 'Sooner or later I'm going to tell Junior a few home-truths.'

'We'd all like to do that,' said Julian. 'But let's hold our horses till a good moment comes – I don't want that nice Mrs Philpot upset – and you know, if we caused her to lose the two Americans she might suffer badly – in her pocket! I bet they pay well.'

'Well – *I* understand all that too, Ju,' said George.

'But Timmy doesn't. He's longing to have a go at Junior!'

'And how I share that feeling!' said Dick, rubbing Timmy's big head. 'What's the time? Shall we go for a walk?'

'No,' said Julian. 'My legs feel stiff with cycling up so many Dorset hills today. I vote we just stroll around a bit, not go for miles.'

The Five set off together, wandering round the farm buildings. They were all very old, some of them falling to pieces. The roofs had great Dorset tiles, made of stone, uneven and roughly shaped. They were a lovely grey, and were brilliant with lichen and moss.

'Aren't they gorgeous?' said George, stopping to look at the tiles on a small outhouse. 'Look at that lichen, did you ever see such a brilliant orange? But what a pity – half of them have gone from this roof, and someone has replaced them with horrid new tiles!'

'Maybe the Philpots sold them,' said Julian. 'Old tiles like that, brilliant with lichen, can fetch quite a bit of money–especially from Americans. There's many a barn out in America covered with old tiles from this country, moss and all. A bit of old England!'

'If I had a lovely old place like this I wouldn't sell one single tile, or one single bit of moss!' said George, quite fiercely.

'Maybe you wouldn't,' said Dick. 'But some would – if they loved their farm enough and didn't want to see it go to pieces for lack of money. Their fields would be worth more than old tiles to them!'

'I bet old Grandad wouldn't sell them if he could help it!' said Anne. 'I wonder if the American has tried to buy any of these tiles? I guess he has.'

They had an interesting time wandering round.

They found one old barn-like shed stacked with ancient castaway junk, and Julian rummaged in it with great interest.

'Look at this giant cartwheel!' he said, peering into a dark corner. 'It's almost as tall as I am! My word – they must have made all their own wheels here in the old days – in this very shed, perhaps. And maybe their own tools too. Look at *this* old tool – what in the *world* is it?'

They gazed at the curious curved tool, still as strong and as good as it had been two or three centuries before. It was heavy and Julian thought that he wouldn't have liked to use it for more than ten minutes at a time!

'But I bet old Grandad could use it for a whole day and never get tired,' he said. 'When he was a young man, I mean. He must have been as strong as an ox, then.'

'Well, you remember what the girl at the dairy said,' put in Anne. 'She said he had once fought a bull and knocked it out. We must ask him about that. I bet he'd love to tell us.'

'He's a real old character!' said Julian. 'I like him, shouts and temper and all. Come on – it's getting latish. We didn't ask about the evening meal. I wonder what time we ought to get back for it?'

'Half past seven,' said George. 'I asked. We'd better go back now, because we'll have to get ourselves clean – and Anne and I want to help lay the table.'

'Right. Back we go,' said Julian. 'Come on, Tim. Stop sniffing about that old rubbish. Surely you can't smell anything exciting there!'

They went back to the farmhouse, and the girls went to wash at the kitchen sink, seeing Mrs Philpot already preparing for supper. 'Won't be a minute!'

called Anne. 'We'll do those potatoes for you, Mrs
Philpot. I say, what a lovely farm this is. We've been
exploring those old sheds.'

'Yes – they need clearing out,' said Mrs Philpot,
who looked better for the rest she had had. 'But old
Great-Grandad, he won't have them touched. Says he
promised *his* Grandad not to let them go to anyone!
But we did sell some of those lovely old grey tiles once
– to an American, of course, a friend of Mr Henning's,
and Grandad almost went out of his mind. Shouted
day and night, poor old chap, and went about with a
pitchfork in his hand all the time, daring any stranger
even so much as to walk over the fields! We had such a
time with him.'

'Good gracious!' said Anne, having a sudden vision
of the grand old man stalking about his fields, shouting, and waving a great pitchfork.

Supper was really a very pleasant meal, for Mr
Henning and Junior didn't come in. There was much
talk and laughter at the table, though the twins, as
usual, said hardly anything. They puzzled Anne. Why
should they be *so* unfriendly? She smiled at them once
or twice, but each time they turned their eyes away.
Snippet lay at their feet, and Timmy lay under the
table. Great-Grandad was not there, nor was Mr
Philpot.

'They're both making the best of the daylight,' said
Mrs Philpot. 'There's a lot to do on the farm just now.'

The children enjoyed the meat-pie that Mrs Philpot
had baked, and the stewed plums and rich cream that
followed. Anne suddenly yawned a very large yawn.

'Sorry!' she said. 'It just came all of a sudden. I don't
know why I feel so sleepy.'

'You've set *me* off now,' said Dick, and put his hand
in front of an even larger yawn. 'Well, I don't wonder

we feel sleepy. Ju and I set off at dawn this morning –
and I know you girls had a jolly long bus ride!'

'Well, you go to bed, all of you, as early as you like,'
said Mrs Philpot. 'I expect you'll want to be up bright
and early in the morning. The Harries are always up
about six o'clock – they just will *not* stay in bed!'

'And what time does Junior get up?' asked George
with a grin. 'Six o'clock too?'

'Oh, not before nine o'clock, usually,' said Mrs
Philpot. 'Mr Henning comes down about eleven – he
likes his breakfast in bed. So does Junior.'

'WHAT? You don't mean to say you take breakfast up
to that lazy little pest?' said Dick, astounded. 'Why
don't you go and drag him out by the ankles?'

'Well – they are guests and pay well for being here,'
said Mrs Philpot.

'*I'll* take Junior his breakfast,' said George, much to
everyone's astonishment. 'Timmy and I together.
We'd like to. Wouldn't we, Timmy?'

Timmy made a most peculiar noise from under the
table. 'That sounded like a *laugh* to me,' said Dick.
'And I'm not surprised! I'd just like to see Junior's face
if you and Tim walked in on him with his breakfast!'

'Do you bet me I won't do it?' demanded George,
really on the defensive now.

'Yes. I do bet you,' said Dick at once. 'I bet you my
new pocket-knife you won't!'

'Taken!' said George. Mrs Philpot looked puzzled.
'No, no, my dears,' she said. 'I can't have one guest
waiting on another. Though I must say those stairs are
a trial to my legs, when I'm carrying up trays!'

'*I'll* take up Junior's tray *and* Mr Henning's too,
if you like,' said George, in a half-kind, half-fierce
voice.

'NOT Mr Henning's,' said Julian, giving George a

warning look. 'Don't go too far, old thing. Just
Junior's tray will be enough.'

'All right, all right,' said George, rather sulkily.
'Aren't Junior and Mr Henning coming in to supper?'

'Not tonight,' said Mrs Philpot, in a thankful voice.
'They're dining at some hotel in Dorchester, I think. I
expect they get a bit tired of our simple farmhouse
meals. I only hope they won't be too late back. Great-
Grandad likes to lock up early.'

The children were really glad when the evening
meal was cleared away and washed up, for they all felt
heavy with sleep. The good strong air, the exciting
day and the many jobs they had done had really tired
them.

'Goodnight, Mrs Philpot,' they said, when everything was done. 'We're off to bed. Are the twins
coming too?'

The twins actually condescended to nod. They
looked tired out. Julian wondered where Mr Philpot
and old Great-Grandad were – still out working, he
supposed. He yawned. Well, he was for bed – and even
if he had had to sleep on the bare ground that night, he
knew he would sleep well! He thought longingly of his
camp bed.

They went their various ways – the twins and Julian
and Dick to the big barn – the girls upstairs to the room
opposite Junior's. George peeped into it. It was even
untidier than before, and obviously Junior must have
been eating nuts up there, for the floor was strewn
with shells.

They were soon in bed – the girls together in the big,
rather hard, old bed, the boys in their separate camp
beds. Timmy was on George's feet, and Snippet slept
first on one twin's feet, and then on the other's. He was
always perfectly fair in his favours!

A crashing noise awoke the girls about two hours later, and they sat upright in bed, alarmed. Timmy began to bark. George crept to the top of the stairs, hearing Grandad's loud voice below, and then crept back to Anne.

'It's Mr Henning and Junior come back,' she said. 'Apparently old Grandad had locked up, and they crashed and banged on the knocker. My, what a to-do! Here comes Junior!' And indeed, here Junior did come, stamping up the stairs and singing loudly.

'Little pest!' said George. 'Wait till I take him his breakfast tomorrow!'

6 A little excitement for breakfast

It was fun to sleep in the barn. Dick tried to keep awake for a while, and enjoy the barn smell, and the sight of the stars in the sky seen through the open door, where a cool little night breeze came wandering in.

Julian fell asleep at once, and did not even hear the crashing of the knocker at the front door of the farmhouse when the Hennings came in, or the loud voices. He awoke with a start at about one o'clock in the morning, and sat straight up in bed, his heart beating fast. What on earth was that noise he had heard?

He heard it again and laughed. 'What an ass I am! It's only an owl. Or maybe more than one. And gosh, what was that high little scream? A mouse – or a rat? Perhaps the owls are hunting in here?'

He lay still and listened. He suddenly felt a rush of cool air over his face, and stiffened. That must have been an owl's soft-feathered wings! Owls' wings made no noise, he knew. The feathers were so soft that not even a quick-eared mouse could hear an owl swooping silently down!

There came another little high-pitched squeak. The owl's doing his job well, thought Julian. What a fine hunting place for him – a barn where food stuffs are stored – overrun with mice and rats, of course. I bet this owl is worth his weight in gold to the farmer. Well, owl, do your job – but for goodness sake don't

mistake my nose for a mouse! Ah – there you go again
– just over my head. I saw you then – a shadow passing
by!'

He fell asleep once more and didn't wake until the
sun streamed into the barn, lighting up hundreds of
tiny motes floating in the air. Julian looked at his
watch.

'Half past seven! And I meant to be up at seven.
Dick! Wake up!'

Dick was so sound asleep that he didn't wake even
when Julian shook him. He merely rolled over and
settled down again. Julian glanced across the barn, and
saw that the twins' camp beds were empty. They had
stacked their pillows and bedclothes in neat piles, and
disappeared silently out of the door. Without waking
us! thought Julian, pulling on his socks. I wonder if I
can wash at the big kitchen sink. 'Dick – *will* you wake
up?' he said loudly. 'It might be TEN O'CLOCK for all
you care!'

Dick heard the two shouted words and sat up at
once, looking aghast. 'Ten o'clock? Oh *no*! Gosh, I
must have slept all round the clock, Oh, I *say* – I didn't
mean to be late for breakfast. I . . .'

'Calm down,' grinned Julian, brushing his hair. 'I
only said, "It might be ten o'clock for all you care!"
Actually, it's just gone half past seven.'

'Thank goodness for that,' said Dick, lying back in
bed. 'Oh for ten minutes more!'

'The twins have gone already,' said Julian. 'I
wonder if the girls are up. Oh, my goodness, what's
that?'

Something had jabbed him sharply in the back,
making him jump violently. Julian swung round,
expecting it to be Junior or one of the twins playing a
silly joke.

'Oh – it's *you* – Nosey the jackdaw!' he said, looking at the cheeky bird, now perched on his pillow. 'You've got a jolly sharp beak!'

'Chack!' said the jackdaw, and flew to his shoulder. Julian felt flattered – until the jackdaw pecked his ear! 'Here – you take the bird,' he said to the unwary Dick, and handed Nosey to him. Nosey promptly pounced on the watch lying beside Dick's pillow and flew off with it. Dick gave an angry yell.

'Bring that back, you crazy bird! Don't you know a watch when you see one? He's taken my watch, Ju – goodness knows where he'll hide it!'

'He's gone into the roof,' said Julian. 'We'd better tell the twins. Perhaps they can deal with him. Now WHY doesn't he take Junior's watch – that would be a trick I should *really* applaud!'

'CHACK, CHACK, CHACK,' said Nosey, exactly as if he agreed. He had to open his beak to say 'chack' and the watch promptly fell out. It bounced on to a sack far below, and the bird swooped down to get it. Dick also swooped, and as the watch had now slipped between two sacks, he managed to get it before the jackdaw.

Nosey flew up into the roof, and 'chacked' angrily. 'Don't use such bad language,' said Dick severely, strapping on his watch. 'You ought to be ashamed of yourself!'

They went out of the barn and round to the farmhouse. There were sounds of people about, and the two boys felt quite ashamed of being so late! Breakfast was on the table, but already quite a number of people seemed to have had it!

'The girls haven't had theirs,' said Dick, looking at the places set in front of the chairs where George and Anne had sat the night before. 'But the twins have. It looks as if *everyone* has, except us four, apparently! Ah

– here's Mrs Philpot. Sorry we're late. We overslept, I'm afraid.'

'That's all right!' said Mrs Philpot, smiling. 'I don't expect my visitors to be up early. Anyone can sleep late on a holiday!'

She held a tray in her hands, and set it down on the table. 'That's for Mr Henning – he'll ring when he wants his breakfast. That's Junior's tray over there. I make the coffee when they ring,' she said, and went out again.

There was cold ham for breakfast, boiled eggs and fruit. The two boys tucked in, and looked round reprovingly when the two girls came, with Timmy behind them, still sleepy-eyed. 'Overslept, I suppose?' said Dick, pretending to be shocked. 'Sit down. I'll pour you some coffee?'

'Where's Junior – not down yet, I hope?' said George anxiously. 'I haven't forgotten my bet about taking up his breakfast!'

'I say – do you think it's all right to let George take up Junior's breakfast?' said Julian, after a pause. 'George, don't throw the tray at him or anything, will you?'

'I might,' said George, eating a boiled egg. 'Anything to get your new pocket-knife from you!'

'Well, don't go too far teasing Junior,' said Julian warningly. 'You don't want to make the Henning family walk out and leave Mrs Philpot high and dry!'

'All right, all right,' said George. 'Don't nag. I think I'll have another egg, Dick. Pass one over, please. I don't know why I'm so hungry.'

'Leave a bit of room for this ham,' said Dick, who had cut himself two good slices. 'It's out of this world! Simply too good to be true! I could eat it all day.'

The two girls tucked into their breakfast, and just as

they were finishing, a bell rang very loudly in the
kitchen, jangling just above their heads. They jumped
violently. Mrs Philpot came into the room at once.
'That's Mr Henning's bell,' she said. 'I must make his
coffee.'

'I'll take up his tray,' said Anne. 'George is going to
take up Junior's.'

'Oh no – I *really* don't like you to do that,' said Mrs
Philpot, distressed. Just then another bell rang. It
jangled to and fro for a very long time.

'That's Junior's bell,' said Mrs Philpot. 'He always
seems to think I'm quite deaf!'

'Bad-mannered little beast!' said Dick, and was
pleased to find that Mrs Philpot didn't disagree!

Anne waited till Mr Henning's tray was ready, and
then firmly put her hands to the sides. '*I'm* going to
take it to Mr Henning,' she said in a most determined
voice, and Mrs Philpot smiled gratefully and let her lift
it. 'Bedroom on the left of the stairs, first floor!' she
said. 'And he likes his curtains pulled, too, when his
breakfast is brought.'

'And does Junior like *his* pulled as well?' inquired
George, in such a sugary voice that the two boys
looked round at her suspiciously. What was she up to
now?

'Well – I do pull them for him,' said Mrs Philpot,
'but don't *you* pull them if you don't feel like it! Thank
you very much, dear!'

Anne had already gone upstairs with Mr Henning's
tray, and now George set off with Junior's. She
winked at Dick. 'Get that pocket-knife ready for me!'
she said, and disappeared through the door, grinning
wickedly. She went carefully upstairs with Timmy
close at her heels, wondering whatever George was
doing with a tray!

George came to Junior's door. It was shut. She gave it a violent kick and it flew open. She entered, clattering with her feet, and set the tray down on a table with a jolt that upset the coffee. She went whistling to the windows, and pulled the curtains back across the poles so that they made a loud clattering noise.

Junior had apparently fallen asleep again, his head under the clothes. George upset a chair with a crash. That made Junior sit up, half scared. 'What's going on here?' he began. 'Can't you bring my breakfast without . . .' Then he saw that it was George in the room, not the kindly Mrs Philpot.

'Get out!' he said angrily. 'Crashing about like that! Pull the curtains across again. The sun's too strong. And look how you've spilt the coffee! Why didn't Mrs Philpot bring my breakfast? She usually does. Here – put the tray on my knees, like she does!'

George whipped the bed clothes off him, took up the tray and set it down violently on his pyjamaed knees. The hot coffee got a violent jerk and some drops fell on to his bare arm. They were hot, and he yelled loudly. He lashed out at George, and hit her hard on the shoulder.

That was a very great mistake. Timmy, who was at the door watching, leapt on to the bed at once, growling. He pulled the terrified boy on to the floor, and kept him lying there, standing over him, deep growls coming from the depths of his great body.

George took absolutely no notice. She went round the room, humming a little tune, putting this and that straight, tidying the dressing-table, not seeming to notice what Timmy was doing. She shut the door so that no one would hear Junior's howls.

'George – take this dog off me!' begged Junior. 'He'll kill me! GEORGE! I'll tell my Pop on you. I'm

sorry I hit you. Oh, DO take this dog off me, PLEASE
do!'

He began to weep, and George looked scornfully
down at him. 'You nasty spoilt little pest,' she said.
'I've a good mind to leave you here all morning, with
Timmy on guard! But this time I'll be generous to
you. Come here, Tim. Leave that funny little worm
there on the floor!'

Junior was still weeping. He crept into bed and
wrapped the blankets round him. 'I don't want any
breakfast,' he wept. 'I'll tell Pop about you. He'll get
you all right.'

'Yes, you tell him,' said George, tucking him in so
tightly that he couldn't move. 'You tell him – and I'll
whisper into Timmy's ear that you've told tales on me
– and honestly, I simply don't know what *he'll* do!'

'You are the most horrible boy I've ever met,' said
Junior, knowing when he was beaten. George
grinned. So he thought she was a boy, did he? Good!

'Mrs Philpot isn't going to bring up your breakfast
any more,' she said. '*I'm* going to – with Timmy. See?
And if you dare to ring that bell more than once each
morning, you'll be sorry!'

'I don't *want* my breakfast brought up,' said Junior,
in a small voice. 'I'd rather get up and go downstairs
for it. I don't *want* you to bring it.'

'Right. I'll tell Mrs Philpot,' said George. 'But if
you change your mind, just tell me. I'll bring it up any
morning – with Timmy!'

She went out and banged the door, Timmy trotting
down the stairs in front of her, puzzled but pleased. He
didn't like Junior any more than George did.

George went into the kitchen. Dick and Julian were
still there. 'You've lost your bet, Dick,' said George.
'Pocket-knife, please. I not only took up his breakfast,

and accidentally spilt hot coffee on him, but Timmy here pulled him out of bed and stood over him, growling. What a sight that was! Poor Junior doesn't want his breakfast in bed any more! He's coming down for it each morning.'

'Good for you, George!' said Dick, and slid his pocket-knife across the table. 'You deserve to win. Now – sit down and finish *your* breakfast and mind – I'm not betting anything else for a long, long time!'

7 The twins change their minds

The twins, Harry and Harriet, had had their breakfast some while ago. They now came into the big kitchen, Snippet at their heels, and scowled to see the Five *still* having breakfast there. Anne was in fits of laughter over George's account of the way she dealt with Junior.

'You *should* have seen his face when I plonked the breakfast tray on his knees, and the hot coffee splashed him!' said George. 'He let out a yell that startled even old Timmy. And when he hit me, and Timmy leapt on the bed and dragged him out on to the floor, his eyes nearly fell out of his head!'

'No wonder he's decided to come down to breakfast each morning, then,' said Julian. 'He'll be scared stiff of you appearing with a breakfast tray again!'

The twins listened to this in amazement. They looked at one another, and nodded. Then they walked up to the breakfast table, and for once, only one twin spoke. Whether it was Harry or Harriet, nobody knew, for they both looked so much alike.

'What's happened?' said the twin to George. 'Why did *you* take up Junior's breakfast tray?'

'Because we were all so fed up with the way Junior – and his Pop – impose on your mother,' said George. 'Fancy a *boy* having breakfast in bed!'

'So old George took it into her head to take up his breakfast herself, and said she'd teach him such a lesson he'd be a bit more considerate of your mother in future,' said Dick. 'What's more, I was idiotic enough to bet George she wouldn't do it – and now she's won my best pocket-knife off me – look!'

George proudly displayed the knife. The twins each gave a sudden loud laugh, which surprised the others very much. 'Well!' said Dick. 'Fancy you being able to *laugh*! You always look so fierce and unfriendly. Well, now that you've condescended to talk to us, let me tell you this – we think your mother is absolutely tops, and far from giving her more trouble, we're all going to help as much as we can. Got that?'

Both twins were smiling broadly now. They took it in turns to speak, which was really much more friendly than their usual stiff way of talking in unison.

'We hate Junior!' said one twin. 'He thinks our mother is a kind of slave, to come when he rings for her, or shouts for her.'

'His father's the same,' said the other twin. 'Wanting this and that, and sending our mother all over the place to fetch and carry for him. Why doesn't he go and stay at a hotel?'

'He doesn't because he's so set on snooping out our old things and buying them,' said the other twin. 'I know for a fact that Mother has sold him some of her own things – but she just *had* to have some money; things are so expensive, and we grow out of our clothes so quickly.'

'It *is* nice to hear you talking properly,' said Julian, clapping the twin on the back. 'And now would you mind letting us know how to tell which of you is which? I know one's a boy and one's a girl, but you both look exactly alike to me – you might be two boys!'

The twins gave sudden, mischievous grins. 'Well –
don't you tell Junior, then,' said one. 'You can always
tell *me* by this scar on my hand, see? Harriet hasn't any
scar. I'm Harry.'

The four looked at the long thin scar on the boy's
hand. 'I got that by tearing the back of my hand on
barbed wire,' said Harry. 'Now you'll know us from
each other! But tell us all about George and the
breakfast tray, from beginning to end. Good old
George. She looks just as much a boy as Harriet
does.'

It was very pleasant to find the twins so friendly,
after their stiff, sullen dislike. The four warmed to
them – and when Mrs Philpot suddenly appeared in
the kitchen to clear away breakfast, she was astounded
to see her twins talking and laughing happily with the
others. She stood and stared, a delighted smile on her
face.

'Mother! Junior's not going to have breakfast in bed
any more!' said Harry. 'Listen why!' And the story had
to be told all over again. George went red. She was
afraid that Mrs Philpot would be displeased. But no,
she threw back her head and laughed.

'Oh, that really does me good,' she said. 'But I hope
Junior doesn't tell his father, and they don't both go off
in a hurry! We do need their money, you know, much
as I hate having them here. Now I *must* clear away
breakfast!'

'No, you mustn't. That's *our* job,' said Anne. 'Isn't
it, twins?'

'YES!' said both twins together. 'We're all friends
now, Mother – let them belong to the family.'

'Well, I'll go and see to the chickens, then, if you're
going to clear away,' said Mrs Philpot. 'You can wash
up, too, bless you!'

'Look – how would you like to go round the farm in our old Land Rover today?' said Harry to the others. 'It's the best way to see over the farm. I think Bill's got to go round this morning, and check on the fields and the stock. He'll take you, if I ask him.'

'Fine!' said Julian. 'What time?'

'In about half an hour,' said Harry. 'I'll find Bill – and when you hear a horn hooting, come on out. By the way, Bill isn't much of a talker, but if he takes to you, he'll be quite pally.'

'Right,' said Julian. 'Can Dick and I do something while the others are clearing away?'

'Gosh yes, there's ALWAYS something to do on a farm,' said Harry. 'Come on up to the chicken-houses – Harriet and I are patching them up to stop the rain leaking in.'

Julian and Dick, with Timmy behind them, immediately went off with the twins, now as merry and friendly as before they had been dour and sullen! What a change!

'Well, thank goodness I took Junior's breakfast up to him, and put him in his place,' said George, folding up the tablecloth. 'It was apparently just the one thing that would make the twins friendly! Listen, Anne, I believe that's Junior coming.'

She slipped behind the dresser, while Anne set the chairs straight round the table. Junior came creeping in very quietly indeed, and looked round fearfully. He seemed very relieved to find only Anne there. He considered that she was *quite* harmless!

'Where's that dog?' he asked.

'What dog?' said Anne innocently. 'Snippet?'

'No – that great ugly mongrel – and that awful boy he belongs to,' said Junior, still fearful.

'Oh, you mean George, I suppose,' said Anne,

amused that Junior thought George was a boy. 'Well, look over there!'

Junior saw George advancing on him from behind the dresser, gave one agonised yell and fled, fearing that she had Timmy behind her. George laughed.

'We shan't have much trouble with *him* in future,' she said. 'I just hope he doesn't say too much to his Pop!'

After a while they heard the sound of a hooter outside. 'That's the Land Rover,' said George, excited. 'Well, we've just finished the washing-up. Hang up the teacloths to dry, Anne. I'll pop these dishes into the cupboard . . .'

Soon they were out of the great kitchen door and down the passage that led to the yard. Not far off was a van-like car, the Land Rover. It was an old one, very dirty, and a bit lopsided. Dick and Julian yelled to the girls.

'Buck up! Didn't you hear us hooting?'

The girls ran to the Land Rover. Bill, the farm hand, was at the wheel. He grinned at them and nodded. Timmy greeted George as if he hadn't seen her for a year and almost knocked her down in his playfulness.

'Tim! Don't be so silly!' said George. 'Planting your great muddy paws all over me! Where are the twins? Aren't they coming?'

'Naw,' said Bill. 'They be busy.'

They all got in, and were just about to set off when someone else appeared. 'Wait! I'm coming! Wait, I say!'

And up ran Junior, full of himself as usual. 'Jump down, Tim – go to him,' said George, in a low voice. And very willingly indeed Timmy leapt down and ran straight towards the unsuspecting Junior. He gave one loud yell, turned, and fled for his life.

'Well, that's got rid of *him*!' said Dick, with much satisfaction. 'Look at Timmy – he's laughing all over his hairy old face! You love a joke, don't you, Tim?'

It did indeed look as if Tim was laughing, for he had his mouth wide open, showing all his teeth, and his tongue was hanging out happily. He leapt back into the car.

'Sensible dog, that,' said Bill, and then relapsed into his usual silence as he started up the Land Rover with a really shattering noise. It moved off towards the fields.

How it jolted! The four clung to the sides of the van, almost bumped off their seats as the Land Rover jerked its way over field paths, up hill and down hill, jolting in and out of deep ruts, appearing to be on the point of overturning at any minute. Anne wasn't sure that she liked it much, but the others enjoyed every minute.

'Now you'll see the farmland,' said Bill, as they came to the top of the hill. 'Look yonder! Could be the finest farm in the country, if Mr Philpot had the money!'

8 All round the farm

The Five thoroughly enjoyed their ride over the big
farm. It spread out in all directions over undulating
hills, and the van swung up and down and continually
lurched round corners. It stopped every now and again
so that the children might see the magnificent views.

Bill told them the names of the great fields as they
passed them. 'That's Oak Tree Field – that's Hangman's Copse over there – that's Tinkers' Wood Field –
and that's Faraway Field – the farthest from the farmhouse.'

Name after name came from his lips, and it seemed
as if the sight of the fields he knew and loved suddenly
set his tongue going. He told them about the stock
too. 'They're the new cows over there – give good
milk they do – helps a farmer no end to get money
every week for milk, you know. And they're the bulls,
down in that field. Fine creatures, too – cost a mint of
money. But Mr Philpot, he believes in good animals.
He'd rather go without a new car than buy poor stock.
They're the sheep right away over there – see, dotted
about on those slopes. Can't take you to see 'em today,
though. You'd like Shepherd. He's been here so long,
and is so old, he knows every inch of the farm!'

He relapsed into silence after his unusual spate of
talk, and turned down a path that took the children
back towards the farmhouse, using a different route,
to show them even more fields.

There were glorious fields of corn, golden in the sun, waving in the breeze with a wonderful rustling noise. 'I could sit here for hours and look at that, and listen,' said Anne.

'Then don't you marry a farmer, if you want to do that, for a farmer's wife has no time to sit!' said Bill dryly, and was silent again.

They jolted along, shaken to the bones, but loving every minute. 'Cows, calves, sheep, lambs, bulls, dogs, ducks, chickens,' chanted Anne. 'Corn, kale, beet, cauliflower – ooh, Bill, look out!'

The van had gone at such speed into a deep rut that Anne was nearly flung out. Timmy shot through the back entrance of the van, and landed on the ground, rolling over and over. He got slowly to his feet, looking most amazed.

'Timmy! It's all right! It was only a bigger hole than usual!' shouted George. 'Buck up – jump in!'

As the Land Rover didn't stop, Timmy had to gallop after it, and enter with a flying leap from the back. Bill gave a snort of laughter, which made the wheel wobble dangerously. 'This old car's almost human,' he said. 'Just jigs about for joy on a day like this!'

And he drove headlong over a slanting path and straight down into a hollow, making poor Anne groan again. 'All very well for Bill!' she said, in Julian's ear. '*He's* got the wheel to hang on to!'

In spite of the jolting and bumping the Five enjoyed their ride round the farm immensely. 'Now, we really know what it's like!' said Julian, as the Land Rover came to a very sudden stop near the farmhouse, throwing them all on top of one another. 'My word – no wonder old Great-Grandad and Mr and Mrs Philpot love the place. It's GRAND! Thanks awfully, Bill.

We've enjoyed it tremendously! Wish *my* family had a farm like this!'

'Farm like this? Ay. It's taken centuries to grow,' said Bill. 'All the names I told you – they're centuries old too. Nobody knows now who was hanged down in Hangman's Copse – or what tinkers came to Tinkers' Wood. But they're not forgot as long as the fields are there!'

Anne stared at Bill in wonder. Why, that was almost poetry, she thought. He turned and saw her gazing at him. He nodded at her.

'You understand all right, miss, don't you?' he said. 'There're some that don't, though. That Mr Henning, he raves about it all – but he don't understand a thing. As for that boy of his!' And to Anne's surprise he turned and spat into the ditch. 'That's what I think of *him*!'

'Oh – it's just the way he's been brought up, I expect,' said Anne. 'I've met heaps of fine American children, and . . .'

'Well, *that* one wants a hiding!' said Bill, grimly. 'And if it wasn't that Mrs Philpot begged me to keep my hands off him, he'd be black and blue, that boy! I tell you! Trying to ride on the nervy calves and chasing the hens till they're scared off egg-laying – and stoning the ducks, poor critters – and slitting sacks of seed just for the fun of seeing it dribble out and waste! Hoo, wouldn't I like to shake him till his bones rattled!'

The four listened in silence, horrified. Junior was much worse than they had thought, then. George felt very very pleased that she had taught him a lesson that morning.

'Don't you worry any more about Junior,' said Julian grimly. '*We'll* keep him in order while we're here!'

They said goodbye and walked back to the farm-house, stiff and sore from the bumpy, bone-shaking ride, but with their minds full of the lovely sloping hills, the blue distance, the waving corn, and the feel of a farmland in good heart.

'That was good,' said Julian, voicing the feelings of the others. 'Very good. I somehow feel more English for having seen those Dorset fields, surrounded by hedges, basking in the sun.'

'I like Bill,' said Anne. 'He's so – so solid and real. He *belongs* to the land, just as the land belongs to him. They're one!'

'Ah – Anne has discovered what farming really means!' said Dick. 'I say, I'm starving, but I really don't like to go and ask for anything at the farmhouse. Let's go down to the village and get buns and milk at the dairy.'

'Oh *yes!*' said Anne and George, and Timmy gave a few sharp, short barks as if he thoroughly agreed. They set off down the lane that led to the village, and soon came to the little ice-cream shop, half baker's half dairy. Janie, the small talkative girl, was there again. She smiled at them in delight.

'You're here again!' she said, in pleasure. 'Mum's made some macaroons this morning. See – all gooey and fresh!'

'Now how did you guess that we are all very partial to macaroons?' said Dick, sitting down at one of the two little tables there. 'We'll have a plateful, please.'

'What, a *whole* plateful?' exclaimed Janie. 'But there's about twenty on a plate!'

'Just about right,' said Dick. 'And an ice-cream each, please. Large. And don't forget our dog, will you?'

'Oh no, I won't,' said Janie. 'He's a very *nice* dog,

isn't he? Have you noticed what lovely smiley eyes
he has?'

'Well, yes, we have. We know him quite well, you
see,' said Dick, amused. George looked pleased. She
did so like Timmy to be praised. Timmy liked it too.
He actually went up to Janie and licked her hand!

Soon they had a plateful of delicious macaroons in
front of them – and they were indeed nice, and *very*
'gooey' inside, as Janie had so rightly said. George
gave Timmy one, but it was really wasted on him,
because he gave one crunch, and then swallowed it! He
also chased his ice-cream all over the floor again, much
to Janie's delight.

'How do you like it at Mrs Philpot's?' she asked.
'Kind, isn't she?'

'Very!' said everyone together.

'We love being at the farm,' said Anne. 'We've been
all over it this morning, in the Land Rover.'

'Did Bill take you?' asked Janie. 'He's my uncle. But
he don't usually say much to strangers.'

'Well, he said plenty to us,' said Julian. 'He was
most interesting. Does he like macaroons?'

'Oooh yes,' said Janie, rather astonished. 'Everyone
likes Mum's macaroons.'

'Could he eat six, do you think?' asked Julian.

'Ooooh *yes*,' said Janie, still astonished, her blue
eyes opened wide.

'Right. Put six in a bag for me,' said Julian. 'I'll give
them to him in return for a great ride.'

'That's right down nice of you,' said Janie, pleased.
'My uncle's been on Finniston Farm all his life. You
ought to get him to tell you about Finniston Castle
before it was burnt down, and . . .'

'Finniston *Castle*!' exclaimed George, in surprise.
'We went all over the farm this morning, and saw

every field – but we didn't see any ruined castle.'

'Oh no, you wouldn't *see* anything!' said Janie. 'I told you – it was burnt down. Right to the ground, ages ago. Finniston Farm belonged to it, you know. There're some pictures of it in a shop down the road. I saw them, and . . .'

'Now, Janie, Janie, how many times have I told you not to chatter to customers?' said Janie's mother, bustling in, frowning. 'That tongue of yours! Can't you learn that people don't want to hear your chatter, chatter, chatter?'

'We like talking to Janie,' said Julian, politely. 'She's most interesting. Please don't send her away.'

But Janie had fled, red-cheeked and scared. Her mother began to arrange the goods on the counter. 'Let's see now – what did you have?' she said. 'Good gracious, where have all those macaroons gone? There were at least two dozen there!'

'Er – well – we had almost twenty – and the dog helped, of course – and Janie put six in a bag for us – let's see now . . .'

'There were twenty-four on that plate,' said Janie's mother, still amazed. 'Twenty-four! I counted them!'

'And five ice-creams,' said Julian. 'How much is that altogether? Most *delicious* macaroons they were!'

Janie's mother couldn't help smiling. She totted up the bill, and Julian paid. 'Come again,' she said, 'and don't you let that little gas-bag of mine bore you!'

They set off down the street, feeling very pleased with life. Timmy kept licking his lips as if he could still taste macaroon and ice-cream! They walked to the end of the street, and came to the little lane that led up to the farm. Anne stopped.

'I'd like to go and look at the horse-brasses in this

little antique shop,' she said. 'You go on. I'll come later.'

'I'll come in with you,' said George, and she turned to the little shop window. The boys walked on by themselves. 'We'll probably be helping on the farm somewhere!' shouted back Dick. 'So long!'

Just as Anne and George were going into the shop, two people came out and almost bumped into them. One was Mr Henning, the American, the other was a man they hadn't seen before. 'Good morning,' Mr Henning said to them, and went into the street with his friend. Anne and George walked into the dark little shop.

There was an old man there, drumming on the counter, looking quite angry. He gave the two girls such a glare that they felt quite frightened!

'That man!' said the old man, and frowned so fiercely that his glasses fell off. Anne helped him to find them among the clutter of quaint old trinkets on his counter. He fixed them on his nose again and looked sternly at the two girls and Timmy.

'If you've come to waste my time, please go,' he said. 'I'm a busy man, children are no good to me. Just want to nose round and touch this and that and never buy anything! That American boy now – he's . . . ah, but you don't know what I'm talking about, do you? I'm upset. I'm *always* upset when people want to buy our beautiful old things and take them away to a country they don't belong to. Now . . .'

'It's all right, Mr Finniston,' said Anne, in her gentle voice. 'You *are* Mr Finniston, aren't you? I just wanted to look at those lovely old horse-brasses please. I won't bother you for long. We're staying at Finniston Farm, and . . .'

'Ah – at Finniston Farm, did you say?' said the old

man, his face brightening. 'Then you've met my great friend, dear old Jonathan Philpot. My very great friend!'

'Is that Mr Philpot, the twins' father?' said George.

'No, no, no – it's old Great-Grandad! We were at school together,' said the old man, excited. 'Ah – I could tell you some tales of the Finnistons and the castle they once owned. Yes, yes – I'm a descendant of the owners of that castle, you know – the one that was burnt down. Oh, the tales I could tell you!'

And it was just at that moment that the adventure began – the Finniston Farm adventure that the Five were never to forget!

9 A very interesting tale

Anne and George looked at the old man, fascinated, as he talked to them. He stood there behind the counter of his little, dark antique shop, surrounded by things even older than himself, a little, bent old man with only a few hairs on his head. He had a kindly, wrinkled face with eyes so hooded with drooping lids that they seemed to look out through slits.

The two girls were thrilled to hear that old Mr Finniston was actually descended from the long-ago Finnistons, who lived in Finniston Castle.

'Is that why your name's Finniston?' asked Anne. 'Tell us about the castle. We only heard about it for the first time today. But we don't even know exactly whereabouts it stood. I didn't see a single stone when we went round the farm this morning!'

'No, no, you wouldn't,' said Mr Finniston. 'It was burnt right down to the ground, you see – and through the centuries people have taken the old stones for building walls. Ah well – it was a long long time ago!'

'How long?' asked George.

'Let's see now – it was burnt down in 1192 – the twelfth century,' said Mr Finniston. 'Norman times, you know. Ever heard of the Normans? Schooling isn't what it was, I know, so maybe . . .'

'Of *course* we've heard of the Normans!' said George, indignantly. 'Every child knows them! They conquered England, and the first Norman king was William the First, 1066!'

'Hmmm – that's right. You've had *some* schooling then,' said Mr Finniston. 'Well, it was a Norman castle – look, like that one in this picture, see?' And he showed them a copy of an old print. They gazed at the stone castle pictured there.

'Yes. It's a Norman castle,' said George. 'Was Finniston Castle just like that?'

'I've got a copy of an old drawing of it somewhere,' said the old fellow. 'I'll find it and show it to you sometime. A small castle, of course – but a very fine specimen. Well, well, you won't be interested in such details, I know. *How* it was burnt down, I don't know. Can't find out for certain. The story goes that it was attacked at night by the enemy, and there were traitors in the castle itself who set fire to it – and while the castle folk were fighting the fire, the enemy walked in and slew nearly all of them.'

'So the castle was no use for living in after that, I suppose,' said Anne. 'But it's strange there isn't even a stone to be seen anywhere.'

'Oh, but that's where you're wrong!' said Mr Finniston, triumphantly. 'There *are* stones from the castle – all over the farm. But only I and old Great-Grandad know where they are now! There's an old wall with some of the castle stones at the bottom – and there's a well – but no, I mustn't tell you those secrets. You might tell them to the Americans who come here and buy up all our old treasures!'

'We won't! We promise!' said both girls at once, and Timmy thumped his tail on the floor, as if he too agreed.

'Well, maybe Great-Grandad will show you one or two of the old castle stones,' said Mr Finniston. 'But I doubt it – I doubt it! I'll tell you one thing you can see at the farmhouse, though – everybody knows about it, so it's no secret. Have you seen the old kitchen door that leads out into the yard?'

'Yes. That oak door, studded with iron knobs, do you mean?' said Anne at once. 'They're quite fashionable now as front doors in ordinary houses, you know. Surely that farmhouse door isn't a real old one?'

Mr Finniston put his head into his hands and groaned as if he were in pain.

'Fashionable! FASHIONABLE! What will they do next? Surely you can't mix up that fine old door with the trashy copies you've seen in modern houses? What's the world coming to? Couldn't you *feel* that that door was real – was as old as the centuries – and once hung on great hinges in a *castle*? Don't you *know* when things are grand with the weight of years?'

'Well,' said Anne, rather out of her depth, 'I did notice the door – but you see, it's very dark just there, and we really can't see it very clearly.'

'Ah – well – most people go about with their eyes shut half the time!' said Mr Finniston. 'You have a look at that door – feel it – look at the great knocker on it. Think of the old Norman folk who hammered on the door with it, all those ages ago!'

George sighed. This kind of thing didn't interest her as much as it interested Anne. A thought suddenly struck her.

'But Mr Finniston – if the castle was built of *stone* – how was it burnt to the *ground*?' she said. 'What happened?'

'I can't find out,' said Mr Finniston sadly. 'I've been into every old library in the county, and looked up every old book of that period – and I've delved into the old records in Finniston church. As far as I can make out, the castle was stormed by enemies – and, as I said, traitors inside set fire to it at the same time. The floors fell in, and the castle was left blazing from top to bottom. The great walls fell inwards and covered the base – and the Finniston family fled. Lord Finniston was killed – but his Lady took the children and hid them – it's said she hid them in the old chapel, near the barns of the farm. Maybe she took them down a secret underground passage, leading from the dungeons to the old chapel itself.'

'An old *chapel* – is it still there?' asked Anne. 'Or was it burnt too?'

'No – it wasn't burnt. It's still standing,' said Mr Finniston. 'Old Great-Grandad will show you.' He shook his head sorrowfully. 'It's a storehouse for grain now. Sad, sad. But, mind you – it's still full of prayer!'

The girls stared at him, wondering what he meant. They began to think he must be a little mad. He stood with his head bent, saying nothing for a while. Then he looked up.

'Well, that's the story, my dears – and it's not only a story, it's history! It happened eight hundred years ago. And I'll tell you something else . . .'

'What?' asked the two girls.

'That castle had cellars – and dungeons!' said the old man. 'The fire only burnt down to the ground floor, which was made of earth flattened down, not wood, so it wouldn't burn. The cellars and dungeons can't have been destroyed – are they still there, undamaged? That's what's been in my mind all these long years. What was down in those cellars – and *is it still there*?'

He spoke in such a hollow voice that the girls felt quite scared. George recovered herself first. 'But why were the dungeons never uncovered?' she asked. 'I

mean, surely someone must have thought of them and
wondered about them?'

'Well, when the castle fell and the walls collapsed,
any underground entrances must have been completely covered with enormously heavy stones,' said
Mr Finniston, peering at them earnestly. 'The peasants
and farm hands living around couldn't possibly move
them, and maybe they were too scared to, anyhow.
They probably lay there for years, till the wind and
weather broke them up. Then they were taken to build
walls and line wells. But by that time everyone had
forgotten about dungeons. Might have been centuries
later, you see.'

He stood and brooded for a while, and the girls
waited politely for him to go on. 'Yes – everyone
forgot . . . and everyone still forgets,' he said. 'Sometimes I wake up in the night and wonder what's
underground there. Bones of prisoners? Chests of
money? Things stored away by the Lady of the castle?
I wake up and wonder!'

Anne felt uncomfortable. Poor old man! He lived
absolutely in the past! His mind had woven for him a
living fantasy, a story that had no certain foundation,
no real truth. She was sorry for him. She wished she
could go and see the place where the old castle had
once stood! It would be overgrown with grass and
weeds, nettles would wave there, and poppies dance in
the summer. There would probably be nothing at all
to show where once a proud castle had stood, its
towers high against the sky, flags flying along the
battlements. She could almost hear the cries of the
enemy, galloping up on horseback, and the fearful
clash of swords! She shook herself and stood up
straight.

'I'm as bad as this old man!' she thought. 'Imagining

things! But what a *tale*! The others will love to hear it. I wonder if the American knows it.'

'Does that American, Mr Henning, know the old story?' she asked, and the old man straightened up at once.

'Not the whole of it – only what he has heard in the village!' he said. 'He comes here and pesters me. He'd like to bring in men and dig up the whole thing! I know him! He'd buy up all the farm, just for the sake of getting that castle site – if he really *knew* there was something worth having, deep under the ground where it once stood. You won't tell him what I've told you, will you? I've talked too much. I always do when someone's upset me. Ah, to think my ancestors once lived in Finniston Castle – and here I am now, a poor old man in a little antique shop that nobody comes to!'

'Well, *we've* come to it,' said Anne. 'I did want to buy some horse-brasses, but I'll come another time. You're upset now. You go and have a rest!'

They went out of the little shop, almost on tiptoe! 'My word!' said George, thrilled. 'I just can't *wait* to tell the boys! What a story – and it really sounded true, Anne, didn't it? I vote we find out where that old castle really stood, and then go and have a look round. Who knows what we might find! Come along – let's get back to the farm as quickly as we can!'

10 Quite a bit of shouting

Anne and George, with Timmy running in front, went back to the farm to find the boys, but they couldn't see them anywhere and gave up. Then they went indoors and found Mrs Philpot shelling peas. They took over the job at once.

'The boys are still helping to mend the hen-house,' said Mrs Philpot. 'The Harries are pleased to have two more pairs of hands to help them! Something always seems to need repairing! If only we could get a few things we need so badly – a new tractor, for instance. But they cost so much! The barns want mending too, and the hen-houses are almost falling down!'

'I hope the harvest will be good for you,' said Anne. 'That will help, won't it?'

'Oh yes – we'll keep our fingers crossed for fine weather from now on!' said Mrs Philpot. 'Thank goodness the cows are such good milkers! What we should do without our milk money, I really don't know! But there – why should I bother you with *my* troubles when you're here for a nice holiday!'

'You don't bother us – and we think it's awfully nice of you to let us help,' said Anne. 'We shouldn't like it if you didn't!'

The girls had no chance of telling the boys what old Mr Finniston had told them, until the afternoon came. They were up at the hen-houses with the two Harries and Snippet, happily hammering and sawing. Snippet was delighted to have so many people whistling cheerily round him, and busily took bits of wood from one boy to another, under the mistaken impression that he was a great help!

Nosey the jackdaw was there too, but he wasn't nearly so popular as Snippet! He pounced on any bright nail or screw he saw, and flew off with it, heedless of the exasperated shouts that followed him.

'Blow that jackdaw!' said Julian, looking up crossly. 'He's just taken the very nail I wanted! Nosey by name and nosey by nature!'

The twins laughed. They seemed entirely different children now that they were friendly – amusing, helpful and most responsible. Julian and Dick admired them – no work was too hard, no hours were too long, if they could help their mother or father.

'We hated you coming here because we knew it would give Mother so much more work,' said Harry. 'We thought if we were beastly to you, you'd go. But you don't make more work! You help an awful lot. It's fun to have you here.'

'I hope the girls are back,' said Dick. 'I know your mother wants help with the peas – such a lot of people to shell for – let me see – counting in your great-grandad, there will be about a dozen people in to dinner. Whew! I certainly *do* hope the girls are in. Ah – here comes that nosey jackdaw again. Look out, Julian, he's after those screws. Snippet, chase him!'

Away went the tiny poodle after the cheeky jackdaw, barking in his high little voice, thoroughly enjoying having so many children round him. Nosey flew up on to the top of the hen-house, and flapped his wings, chacking rude things in a very loud voice indeed.

Dinner was rather a crowded meal, for everyone was there. Great-Grandad frowned when he saw Mr Henning come in with Junior. Junior strutted to his place at table, giving George his best scowl. However, she was just as good at scowling as Junior, and Mr Henning, who happened to catch sight of her giant-size scowl, had quite a shock.

'Now, now, my boy,' he said to her. 'Why pull such an ugly face?'

Nobody told him that George was a girl. Mrs Philpot was really very much amused. She liked George, and couldn't help thinking she would have made a very good boy indeed!

'Er – Mrs Philpot – would it be all right if I bring a friend to lunch here tomorrow?' asked Mr Henning. 'He's called Durleston – Mr Durleston – and he's a great authority on antiques. He's going to give me some advice. You'll remember that you told me you had a quaint old hole in the wall in one of the bedrooms – where in the old days people used to heat embers for warming-pans, and bricks to put in between the bed-sheets. I thought I . . .'

'You thought you could buy 'em, I suppose!' old Great-Grandad suddenly shouted from his place at the head of the table. He thumped on the cloth with the handle of his knife. 'Well, you ask my permission first, see? This place is still mine. I'm an old man, I'm nearly ninety, but I've still got all my wits about me. I don't like this selling of things that have been in our family for donkey's years! That I don't! And . . .'

'Now, now, Grandad, don't excite yourself,' said Mrs Philpot, in her gentle voice. 'Surely it's better to sell old things that we shall never use, in order to buy new tools, or wood to mend the barns?'

'Why can't we sell 'em to our *own* folks, then?'

shouted Great-Grandad, banging with his fork as well. 'Taking them out of the country! Part of our history, they are! Selling our birthright, that's what we're doing – for a mess of potage! That's out of the Bible, let me tell you, Mr Henning, in case you don't know.'

'SURE I KNOW,' said Mr Henning, getting up and shouting back at Great-Grandad. 'I'm not as ignorant as you seem to think. You ought to be glad that a poor, run-down, back-dated country like Britain has got anything to sell to a fine upstanding one like America! You . . .'

'That's enough, Mr Henning,' said Mrs Philpot, with such dignity that Mr Henning blushed red and sat down in a great hurry. 'Sorry, ma'am,' he said. 'But that old man, he gets under my skin; he sure does! What's gotten into him? All I want is to buy things you want to sell. You want new tractors – I want old junk and I'm willing to pay for it. That's all there is to it – buying and selling!'

'OLD JUNK!' shouted Great-Grandad again, banging with his glass now. 'Do you call that great old cart-wheel you bought OLD JUNK? Why, that's more than two hundred years old! *My* great-grandad made it – he told me so, when I was a mite of a boy. You won't find another wheel like it in England. HOO – that wheel was made before the first American was born! I tell you . . .'

'Now, now, Grandad, you know you'll feel ill if you go on like this,' said Mrs Philpot, and she got up and went to the old man, who was shaking with fury. 'You belong to old times, and you don't like the new times, and I don't blame you. But things change, you know. Calm yourself, and come with me and have a lie-down.'

Surprisingly, the old fellow allowed Mrs Philpot to lead him out of the room. The seven children had all sat silent while the shouting had been going on. Mr Philpot, looking worried, broke his habitual silence and addressed a few words to the equally worried-looking Mr Henning.

'Storm in a teacup,' he said. 'Soon blow over.'

'Hmmmm,' said Mr Henning. 'Spoilt my dinner! Selfish, ignorant, rude old man.'

'He's not,' said one of the twins, in a voice trembling with anger. 'He's . . .'

'Enough, Harry!' said his father, in such a stern voice that Harry subsided at once, but began to grind his teeth to show that he was still angry, making a most remarkable noise at the now silent table. Junior had sat as still as a mouse all the time, scared of the angry old man. Timmy had given a few small growls, and Snippet had shot straight out of the kitchen as soon as Great-Grandad had begun to shout!

Mrs Philpot came back, and sat down, looking sad and tired. Julian began to talk to her about Janie and the macaroons, and soon succeeded in making her smile. She even laughed out loud when George told her that they had six macaroons to give Bill for taking them out in the Land Rover.

'I know those macaroons,' announced Junior. 'I buy about thirty of them a week. They're just wunnerful!'

'Thirty! No wonder you're so pasty-faced, then,' said George, before she could stop herself.

'Aw shucks! Pasty-face yourself!' retorted Junior, feeling safe with his father near him.

He heard a sudden ominous growl under the table, felt hot breath on his leg, and decided to say no more. He had forgotten all about the watchful Timmy!

Julian thought it was about time to have some bright

conversation, and began to tell Mrs Philpot about the
hen-houses and what a good job they were making of
patching them to make them rain-proof. Mr Philpot
listened too, nodded, and actually joined in.

'Yes – you're good with your hands, you boys. I had
a look when I came by. Fine work!'

'Harriet's good, too,' said Harry at once. 'She did
that corner where the rats get in. Didn't you, Harry?'

'*I* wanted to help, Pop, but they shooed me off, like
I was a hen!' said Junior in an aggrieved tone. 'Seems as
if they don't want me around. That makes it pretty
lonely, Pop. Can't I come out with you this afternoon?'

'No,' said Pop, shortly.

'Aw, *c'mon*, Pop,' said Junior, in a whiny voice. 'Aw
shucks, Pop, lemme come!'

'NO!' said Pop, exasperated. Timmy gave a growl
again. He didn't like cross voices. He couldn't imagine
why there was so much quarrelling here, and sat up,
tense and still, until George gave him a gentle push
with her toe. Then he lay down again, his head across
her feet.

Everyone was glad when the meal was over, delicious though the food had been. The girls and Harriet
insisted that Mrs Philpot should go and have a rest
while they did all the clearing away and washing-up.
'Now, try not to be unkind to Junior this afternoon,'
she said, as she went. 'He'll be all alone when his
father's gone. Do let him be with you.'

Nobody answered. They hadn't the least intention
of allowing Junior to be with them. 'Spoilt, bad-
mannered little idiot!' thought George, clearing away
with such vigour that she almost knocked Anne over.

'Julian,' she said in a low voice, catching him at the
door as he went out, 'Anne and I have something

interesting to tell you. Where will you be this afternoon?'

'Up in the hen-houses, I expect,' said Julian. 'We'll watch out for you and Anne. See you in about half an hour.'

Junior had sharp ears. He heard exactly what George had said, and he was full of curiosity at once. What was this interesting thing George wanted to tell the boys? Was it a secret? All right – he'd be on hand somewhere to hear it!

And so, when the girls had finished their work, and set off to the hen-houses, Junior followed discreetly behind! He kept well out of sight until he saw George and Anne disappear into a hen-house, where the others were working – and then he crept to a corner outside and put his ear to a knot-hole in the wood. I'll get my own back now! he thought. *I'll* make them smart for leaving me out of things! Just see if I don't!

11 A most exciting tale

The boys were busy hammering and sawing and the girls sat and waited till the noise died down. Snippet was there, leaping about ridiculously with little bits of wood in his mouth, and Nosey the jackdaw had suddenly taken a fancy to the shavings that now covered the floor, and ran about chacking and picking them up.

Outside the hens clucked and squawked, and not far off the ducks quacked loudly. 'Those are the kind of noises I like to hear,' said Anne, settling herself on a sack in a corner. She raised her voice and shouted above the hammering to Dick. 'WANT ANY HELP, DICK?'

'No thanks,' said Dick. 'We'll just finish this job, then sit down and have a rest, and listen to what you have to say. You sit and watch our wonderful carpentering! Honestly, I'd make pounds a week if I took it up!'

'Look out – Nosey has got your nails again!' shouted George. Timmy leapt up as if he was going to chase Nosey, and the jackdaw promptly flew up to a crossbeam, and sat there chacking with laughter. Timmy thought him a very exasperating bird indeed. He lay down again with a thump.

At last the boys had finished the job they were on, and sat down, rubbing their hands over their wet foreheads. 'Well, now you can tell us your news,' said

Dick. 'Good thing we got rid of that little pest of a Junior – I might have hammered a few nails into him by mistake if he'd come worrying us this afternoon.' He imitated Junior's whining drawl. 'Aw shucks, Pop, lemme come with you!'

Outside, his ear to the hole, Junior clenched his fists. He would willingly have stuck a few nails into Dick at that moment!

George and Anne began to tell the four listening children what old Mr Finniston had told them that morning. 'It's about Finniston Castle,' said Anne. 'The old castle that gave the village its name – and the farm as well. The old fellow who told us about it is called Finniston, too – and will you believe it, he's a descendant of the Finnistons who lived in the castle centuries ago!'

'He seems to have spent most of his life trying to discover everything possible about the old castle,' said George. 'He said he'd delved into old libraries – and into the church records here – anywhere that might help him to piece together the castle's history!'

Outside the hen-house, Junior held his breath so as not to miss a single word. Why – his Pop had told him that he couldn't get *anything* out of that old Mr Finniston at the antique shop – not a word about the castle, and its history, or even where the site was. Then why had he told Anne, and the horrible boy George? Junior felt angry, and listened even more keenly.

'The story goes that the twelfth-century enemies came to attack the castle one night – and there were traitors already inside it who set it on fire, so that the castle folk would be busy trying to put out the fire, and wouldn't be prepared for a fight,' said George. 'The inside of it was burnt down to the ground – and then the great stone walls outside collapsed inwards, and lay in enormous heaps there, covering the place where the castle had stood.'

'Whew!' said Dick, visualising it all. 'What a night that must have been! Everybody killed or burnt, I suppose?'

'No, the Lady of the castle wasn't killed and it is said that she took her children to the little chapel near the farmhouse – we really must go and see that, twins – and they stayed there in safety. Anyway, *some* of the family must have escaped, because it is one of their descendants who keeps that little antique shop – old Mr Finniston!'

'This is tremendously interesting,' said Julian. 'Where's the site of the castle? It should easily be known, because of the great mass of stones that fell there when the walls collapsed.'

'No, they're *not* there now,' said George. 'Mr Finniston said he thought that when the wind and weather had broken them up small enough to be lugged away by the farmers and peasants living nearby, they were taken to build field-walls, or to line wells. He said there were some on this farm. He didn't know himself where the castle once stood because the site would be all grown over, and with no stones left to mark it, it wouldn't be easy to find.'

'But oh, Julian, I *wish* we could find it!' cried Anne, her voice rising in excitement. 'Because, so Mr Finniston says, the cellars and dungeons are probably still there, quite untouched. You see, no one could uncover them for years, because of the heavy stones there – and when the stones were taken away, people had forgotten about the castle and the dungeons!'

'Gosh! So they may *still* be there – with whatever was stored in them hundreds of years ago,' said Dick, thrilled. 'My *word* – there might be priceless things there, as old as the hills! I mean, even an old broken sword would be worth its weight in gold, because it would be so very, very old. I say – don't say a word of all this in front of that American, or he'd dig up the whole farm!'

'We shouldn't *dream* of it,' said George. 'He shan't get to hear a word of this.'

Alas! George little knew that every single word had been overheard by Junior, whose left ear was still pinned to the knot-hole in the wood! His face was red with surprise and delight. WHAT A SECRET! Whatever would his pop say? Dungeons! Perhaps full of gold and jewels and all kinds of things! He rubbed his hands together in delight, thinking that he would soon get even with those annoying children now – as soon as Pop came home, he'd spill everything to him. GEE!

Timmy heard the small sound of Junior rubbing his hands together and sat up, growling, his ears pricked. Snippet growled too, a miniature little sound that nobody took seriously. Timmy then heard Junior creeping away, afraid because he had heard the big dog growling. Timmy growled again and then barked sharply, running to the shut door of the hen-house, scraping at it with his foot.

'Somebody's o tside – quick! If it's Junior, I'll throw him on to the muck-heap!' yelled Dick, and flung open the door. They all trooped out and looked round – but there was nobody there! Junior had shot off at top speed, and was now safely behind the nearest hedge.

'What was it, Tim?' said George. She turned to the others. 'He may have heard those hens scratching near the door,' she said. 'There's no one about. Gosh, I was so afraid that it was that little sneak of a Junior! He'd tell his pop every single thing!'

'Twins, listen – Mr Finniston told us that one of the things that *was* saved from the castle – or found afterwards, perhaps – was a great old oak door, iron-studded,' said Anne, suddenly remembering. 'Is that one of your kitchen doors?'

'Yes – that must be the door leading into the dark little passage,' said Harry. 'You wouldn't have noticed it particularly because it's usually kept open, and it's very dark just there. Gosh, I suppose it *could* have come from the castle. It's enormously thick and strong. I wonder if Dad knows.'

'We'll tell him,' said Harriet. 'I say – shall we go and look for the site of the castle sometime? If only we could find it! Do you suppose that if we found the cellars and dungeons, full of chests and things, they'd belong to *us*? The farm belongs to our family, of course, and all the land around.'

'Does it? Well then, perhaps anything found on this land would be yours!' said Julian.

'We might be able to buy a new tractor!' said the twins, both together, in the same excited voice.

'Let's go and look for the castle site *now*,' said George, her voice sounding so excited that Timmy sat up and barked.

'No. We must finish this job,' said Julian. 'We promised we would. There's plenty of time to hunt around, because nobody knows about this except us.'

Julian was wrong, of course. Junior knew – and Junior meant to tell the whole secret to his father as soon as ever he could! He could hardly wait for him to come home.

'Well, we'd better be getting back to the house,' said George. 'We told Mrs Philpot we'd pick some rasp-berries for supper tonight, so we'd better fetch baskets, and begin. Oh, I do HOPE we find that castle site. I shall dream about it tonight, I know I shall.'

'Well, try and dream where it *is*,' said Julian, with a laugh. 'Then you can lead us straight to it tomorrow morning. I suppose *you* haven't any idea where it might be, have you, twins?'

'No,' they said together, frowning. 'No idea at all!' And Harriet added, 'You see, the farm's so big – and I suppose it might have been built *any*where on our land.'

'Yes – but probably near the top of a hill,' said Julian. 'Castles used to overlook surrounding land, you know, so that approaching enemies could easily be seen. And then again, George said Mr Finniston told them that the Lady of the castle escaped with her children and took them in safety to the chapel, which wouldn't be very far away. I should guess that the castle site must be not further than a quarter of a mile from the chapel, so that narrows the search down a bit. By the way, we really must look at the chapel – it sounds interesting, even though it has been used as a storehouse for years!'

The girls picked raspberries for the rest of the afternoon, and the boys finished their jobs. They went back to the farmhouse for tea, feeling pleasantly tired. The girls were already there, laying the table. They pounced on the twins, and George spoke excitedly.

'Twins! We've been looking at the old studded door. It's MAGNIFICENT! Come and see it, Julian and Dick. If it isn't from the old castle, I'll eat my hat – *and* my shoes as well!'

She took them to the great door that opened from the kitchen into the passage that led to the yard. With much difficulty she swung it shut. They all gazed at it. It had been almost too heavy for George to move!

Great iron studs had been driven into it, so deeply and firmly that only by destroying the door itself could they ever be removed. There was a curious iron handle in the middle of the outer side, and George raised it and brought it down smartly. A loud bang resounded through the kitchen, and made the others jump.

'The knocker that visitors used when they came to the castle, I suppose!' said George, laughing at their surprised faces. 'Noise enough to rouse everyone, and alert any guard at once. Do you suppose it was the *front* door of the castle – it's big enough! It must be worth an enormous sum of money!'

'Look out – there's Junior!' said Anne, in a low voice. 'He's grinning all over his face. What do you suppose he's been up to? I wish I knew!'

12   Really very thrilling

At teatime Julian spoke to Mrs Philpot about the old kitchen door. 'That's a fine old door,' he said. 'Did it come from the castle, do you suppose?'

'Yes – so it's said,' answered Mrs Philpot. 'Great-Grandad here knows more about it than I do, though.'

Great-Grandad was not at the table. He was sitting in his enormous old chair in the window, with Snippet at his feet. He was pulling contentedly at his pipe, a cup of tea on the windowsill beside him.

'What's that?' called the old man. 'Speak up!' Julian repeated what Mrs Philpot had said, and the old fellow nodded.

'Oh ay! That door's from the castle all right. Made of the same oak as the beams in the barns, and the floors of the bedrooms above! Ay, and that American fellow's been at me about it, too! Hoo! Offered me fifty pounds for it. FIFTY POUNDS I wouldn't take a thousand. What – have that old door hanging in some newfangled house out in that American country, wherever it is? NO. I say NO, and I'll say it till I'm blue in the face!'

'All right, Grandad – don't upset yourself,' said Mrs Philpot. She spoke to Julian in a low voice. 'Change the subject, quickly, or Grandad will go on and on, poor old fellow!'

Julian racked his brain for a change of subject, and fortunately remembered the hen-houses. He at once began to tell Great-Grandad all they had done that afternoon, and the old fellow calmed down at once, and listened with pleasure. Snippet, who had run in fright to the twins as soon as Great-Grandad had begun to shout, ran back to him, and settled on his feet. Timmy also decided to join them, and soon Great-Grandad was completely happy again, drawing on his old pipe, with one dog at his feet, the other resting a great head on his knee. Timmy certainly did love Great-Grandad!

Mr Henning did not come back that night, much to everyone's relief, but arrived next day just before lunch, bringing with him a dried-up fellow wearing thick glasses, whom he introduced as Mr Richard Durleston.

'The *great* Mr Durleston!' he said proudly. 'Knows more about old houses in England than anyone else in the country. I'd like him to see that old door after lunch, Mrs Philpot – and the strange opening in the wall of the bedroom upstairs, which was used to heat embers and bricks for warming beds years ago.'

Fortunately Great-Grandad was not there to object, and after they had had dinner, Mrs Philpot took Mr Durleston to the old studded door. 'Ah, yes,' he said. 'Quite genuine. Very fine specimen. I should offer four thousand pounds, Mr Henning.'

How Mrs Philpot longed to accept such an offer! What a difference it would make to her housekeeping! She shook her head. 'You'd have to talk to old Great-Grandad,' she said. 'But I'm afraid he'll say no. Now I'll take you to see the strange old opening up in one of the bedrooms.'

She took Mr Henning and Mr Durleston upstairs, and the four followed, with Timmy. It was indeed a strange opening in the wall! It had a wrought-iron door rather like an old oven door. Mrs Philpot opened it. Inside was a big cavity, which had obviously been used as a kind of oven to heat bricks for placing into cold beds; some of the old bricks were actually still there, blackened with long-ago heating! Mrs Philpot took out what looked like a heavy iron tray with an ornamental raised edge. On it were old, old embers!

'This tray was used for heating and holding the embers before they were put into warming-pans,' she said. 'We still have one old warming-pan left – there on the wall, look.'

The four, just as interested as the two men, looked at the copper warming-pan, glowing red-gold on the wall. 'The red-hot embers were emptied into that,' Mrs Philpot told the children, 'and then the pan was carried by its long handle into all the bedrooms, and thrust into each bed for a few minutes to warm it. And that funny little opening in the wall is, as I said, where people years and years ago heated the embers – and the bricks too, which were wrapped in flannel and left in each bed.'

'Hmmmmm. Very interesting. Quite rare to see one in such a well-preserved state,' said Mr Durleston, peering into the opening through thick glasses. 'You could make an offer for this too, Mr Henning. Interesting old place. We'll have a look at the barns too, I think, and the outbuildings. Might be a few things there you could pick up with advantage.'

George thought it was a good thing the twins were not with them to hear all this. They seemed to share with their great-grandad a hatred of parting with any of the treasures belonging to the old farmhouse!

Mrs Philpot took the two men downstairs again, and the four followed.

'I'll just take Mr Durleston to the old chapel,

ma'am,' said Mr Henning, and Mrs Philpot nodded. She left them and hurried back into the kitchen, where she had a cake baking. The four looked at one another, and Julian nodded his head towards the two men, now making their way out of doors. 'Shall we go too?' he said. 'We haven't seen this chapel yet, either!'

So they followed the two men, and soon came to a tall, quaint old building with small and beautifully arched windows set high up in the wall. They went in at the door, a few paces behind the two men, and stared in wonder.

'Yes – you can see it was once a chapel!' said Julian, instinctively speaking in a low voice. 'Those lovely old windows – that arch there . . .'

'And the *feel* of it!' said Anne. 'I know now what old Mr Finniston down at that little shop meant, when he said that though it was now a storehouse, it was still full of prayer! You can *feel* that people have been here to pray, can't you? What a lovely little chapel. Oh, I do wish it wasn't used as a storehouse!'

'I was told by an old fellow down in the village antique shop that a Lady Phillippa, who was once the Lady of the castle, brought each of her fifteen children here to learn their prayers,' said Mr Durleston, surprisingly. 'Hmm, hmm – nice old story. Probably true. Chapels were often built near to castles. Wonder which path they took from the castle to the chapel. All gone now, no castle, nothing! Hmm, hmm.'

'I'd like to buy this chapel, knock it down, and take it stone by stone to my place in the States,' said the American enthusiastically. 'Fine specimen, isn't it? It would look wonderful in my place.'

'Can't advise that,' said Mr Durleston, shaking his head. 'Not in good taste. Let's go to those outbuildings over there. Might see something in the old junk there.'

They went off, and the children stayed behind, entranced with the little chapel. Sacks upon sacks of grain and what looked like fertiliser were arranged in rows all over the floor. A cat had three kittens cuddled together on one sack, and a dove cooed somewhere high up in the arched roof. It was a very peaceful sound, somehow just right for the silent little place. The children trooped out quietly, not feeling inclined to follow the brash Mr Henning round any more.

'At least the other man stopped him from his mad idea of removing the chapel stone by stone,' said Anne. 'I couldn't *bear* that beautiful old place to be torn up by its roots and replanted somewhere else.'

'You sound quite angry, Anne – almost as fierce as old Great-Grandad!' said Julian, slipping his arm through his sister's. 'I don't somehow think the old chapel will be sold to Mr Henning – even if he offered a million dollars for it!'

'Well, I like most Americans very much,' said Anne. 'But not Mr Henning. He – he wants to buy history just as if it were chocolate or toffee!'

That made the others laugh. 'I say!' said Julian, 'what about having a snoop round, now we're out, and just see if we can decide where to hunt for the site of the castle? I presume we all agree that it can't be *very* far away from the chapel?'

'Yes – that's agreed,' said Dick. 'And it's also agreed that the site is probably on a hill. The snag is that there are rather a lot of hills on this undulating farmland!'

'Let's make our way over there – up the nearest slope,' said George. 'Hallo, here are the twins. We'll call them. They might like to come.'

The twins soon joined them, and said yes, they would certainly like to hunt for the castle site. 'But it might take years!' said Harry. 'It might be anywhere on the farm!'

'Well, we plan to examine this slope first,' said Julian. 'Heel, Tim, heel, Snippet. Oh gosh, here's Nosey the jackdaw too. NOT on my shoulder, if you don't mind, Nosey. I rather value my ears!'

'Chack!' said the jackdaw, and flew to the twins.

They made their way up the slope. There was, however, absolutely nothing to be seen except grass, grass, grass! They came to a big mound and stood looking at it.

'A very *large* mole must have made that!' said Dick, which made them all laugh, for the mound was as high as their shoulders. Rabbit holes could be seen at the bottom, though it was probable that very few burrowed there now – the great rabbit disease, myxomatosis, had wiped them practically out of existence on Finniston Farm.

Timmy couldn't see a rabbit hole without scraping at it, and soon he and Snippet were scattering earth over everyone. Snippet was small enough to disappear into one hole, and came out carrying – of all things – an oyster shell! Julian took it out of his mouth in amazement.

'Look here – an *oyster* shell – and we're miles from the sea. How did it get there? Go in again, Snippet. Scrape hard, Timmy. Buck up! An idea is glimmering in my brain!'

Before long, what with Timmy's excited scraping and Snippet's explorations deep into the burrow, quite a collection of oyster shells, and small and large bones lay on the grass!

'Bones!' said Anne. 'Not bones of *people* surely.

Don't tell me this is a mound covering an old grave or something. Ju.'

'No. But it *is* something rather exciting!' said Julian. 'I'm pretty sure it's an old kitchen-midden.'

'A *kitchen-midden*? What on earth's that?' said George. 'Oh look – Timmy's got another mouthful of oyster shells!'

'A kitchen-midden is what you might call the rubbish-heap of the old days,' explained Julian, picking up some oyster shells. 'It was often very big, when it comprised the rubbish thrown out from large houses – or castles! Things like bones and shells wouldn't rot away like other rubbish – and I do believe we've found the kitchen-midden of the old castle. My word – what a find! Now we know something very important!'

'What?' asked everyone, in excitement.

'Well – we know now that the site of the castle must be somewhere on this slope!' said Julian. 'The kitchen-midden was probably not far from its walls. We're on the scent, scouts, we're on the scent! Come on – let's go further on. Spread out, Examine every inch of the ground!'

13 Junior springs a surprise

The six children felt a sudden surge of excitement, and Timmy felt it too and barked loudly. Snippet joined in, and the jackdaw danced up and down on Harry's shoulder, chacking hoarsely. Junior, who had seen them start out and was tracking them, stared in surprise from behind a bush in a nearby hedge. NOW what was all the excitement about? What had Timmy and Snippet found?

He saw the six children spread out and begin to go slowly up the great slope of the hill. Timmy followed them, rather puzzled. He wished he knew what they were looking for – then he could hunt too! Junior kept safely behind the bush. He knew that if he followed too closely after the children, Timmy would hear him, and bark.

Suddenly the Harries gave a shout. 'Hey!' the others looked up from their search, and saw them beckoning in excitement. 'What about THIS? Come and look!'

Everyone hurried over to the twins, who were standing on a little ridge about two hundred metres below the top of the gently sloping hill. 'Look!' said Harry, sweeping his arm in a circle. 'Would *this* be a likely place for the castle site?'

The four looked at the great shallow depression that the twins pointed to. In shape it was like a very shallow soup plate, certainly big enough for a castle to have been built there! It was covered with thick, closely growing grass, which was a little darker in colour than the grass around.

Julian clapped Harry on the shoulder. 'Yes! I bet this is where the castle once stood! Why should the ground here suddenly have this great depression in it, as if it had sunk down for some reason? The *only* reason could be that some enormously heavy building once stood here – and it *must* have been the castle!'

'It's not too far from the kitchen-midden, where they threw their rubbish, is it?' asked Anne, anxiously, looking back to see how far away that was.

'No – just about right,' said Julian. 'They would be sure to have it some distance away because it would smell, especially in the hot weather. Yes, twins – I think you really have hit on the castle site – and I bet if we had the machinery to excavate here, we'd come across dungeons, cellars, underground passages – and all they contain!'

The twins went red with excitement, and stared solemnly at the great basin-like circle, green with grass. 'What *will* our mother say?' they said, both together.

'Plenty!' said Dick. 'This might be the saving of your farm! But look – let's not say a word about it yet, in case it gets round to Mr Henning. Let's get Bill and ask him if he'll lend us spades and things. We'll tell him we've found some interesting old shells and bones on the hill and want to do a little digging. We'll soon know if this really *is* the site of the castle.'

'Good idea,' said Julian, excited at the thought of being one of the first to dig down into the old dungeons! 'Let's pace round this old site and see how big it is.'

They walked round and round it and decided it was more than big enough for even a large castle. They thought it was strange that the grass should be a different colour there.

'But it does sometimes happen that grass marks out where old buildings once stood,' said Julian. 'I say – this is just about the most exciting thing that ever happened to us – and I'm so glad it was the twins who first recognised the site! After all, it's on their farm!'

'Isn't that Junior running over there?' said George suddenly, as she saw Timmy prick up his ears, and turn his nose to the wind. 'Yes, it is. He's been spying on us, the little beast! There he goes, look!'

'Well, he can't know *much*,' said Julian, gazing after the running figure. 'I don't expect he even knows that a castle was once built here, at the top of this hill – and he certainly wouldn't know we were looking for the site. He's just snooping, that's all.'

But Junior *did* know all about the old castle, for he had overheard the children talking in the hen-house! And he *did* know what they had been looking for! He had followed them as closely as he dared, listening to their shouts – and now he felt that he must get back to his father and tell him what he knew!

He found his father still with Mr Durleston, examining an old fireplace. 'Now that's worth buying,' Mr Durleston was saying. 'You could rip that out, and use it in your own house – a beautiful thing. Very old! And . . .'

'Pop! I say, Pop! Listen!' cried Junior, bursting in. Mr Durleston looked annoyed. That boy again! But Junior took no notice of the old man's annoyance, and pulled urgently at his father's arm. 'Dad! I know where the place is that the castle once stood on! And there's dungeons and cellars underneath, full of treasure, I know there are. Pop, those kids found the place, but they don't know I saw them!'

'What *is* all this, Junior?' said his father, half-annoyed too. 'Silly talk! You don't know anything about castle sites and dungeons and the rest!'

'I do, I do! I heard them all talking in the hen-house – I told you I did!' cried Junior, tugging at his father's sleeve again. 'Pop, they've found an old rubbish-heap too, that belonged to the castle – they called it – a – let me see now – a . . .'

'A midden?' asked Mr Durleston, suddenly taking an interest.

'Yes! That's it. A kitchen-midden!' said Junior triumphantly. 'With bones and shells. And then they looked for where the old castle might have been built – they said it couldn't have been far away, and . . .'

'Well, they were right,' said Mr Durleston. 'A kitchen-midden would certainly pinpoint the castle area! Mr Henning, this is extremely interesting. If you could get permission to excavate, it would be a . . .'

'Oh BOY!' said Mr Henning, interrupting, his eyes almost staring out of his head. 'Can't you see the papers – "American discovers old castle site – unknown for centuries! Excavates dungeons – finds bones of long-ago prisoners – chests of gold coins . . ."'

'Not so fast, not so fast,' said Mr Durleston, disapprovingly. 'There may be nothing at all there. Let us not count our chickens before they're hatched. And mind – not a word to the newspapers, Henning. We don't want a crowd of people rushing to pry over the farm, sending up its price!'

'I didn't think of that,' said Mr Henning, a little cast down. 'All right – we'll go carefully. What do you advise?'

'I should advise you to approach Mr Philpot – *not* the old great-grandad, but the farmer himself – and offer to put down, say, £5,000 for the right to excavate up on the hill there,' said Mr Durleston. 'Then if you strike anything interesting, you can offer a further sum for whatever's down there – say another £5,000. If there *is* anything there, it will be *extremely* valuable – so very, very old. Hmmm. Hmmm. Yes, that is my advice to you.'

'And it sounds pretty good to me,' said Mr Henning, excitement flooding him again. 'You'll stay here and advise me, won't you, Durleston?'

'Certainly, certainly, if you are prepared to pay my fee,' said Durleston. 'I think it would perhaps be advisable if *I* approached Mr Philpot, Mr Henning, not you. You might – er – well – give something away in your excitement. You will come with me, of course – but let me do the talking.'

'Right, old man, you do everything!' said Mr Henning, feeling friendly with the whole world. He clapped the listening Junior on the back. 'Well done, son! You may have let us into something good. Now don't you breathe a word to ANYONE, see?'

'Aw shucks!' said Junior. 'What do you think I am? My mouth's sewn up from now on! Think I'd split, Pop, when there's a chance of getting even with those snooty kids? You go on up that hill when they've gone, and have a look yourself. Mr Durleston will know if it's the real thing or not!'

So, when the six children and dogs were safely out of sight, gone to help with various jobs of work on the farm, Mr Henning and Mr Durleston went with Junior to see the kitchen-midden and the supposed site of the old castle. Mr Henning became very excited indeed, and even the weary-looking Mr Durleston brightened up and nodded his head several times.

'*Looks* the real thing!' he said. 'Yes, we'll get going

this evening – after that fierce old fellow – the old great-grandad – has gone to bed. He might put a spoke in our wheels. He's as old as the hills, but as quick as a jackdaw!'

And so, that evening, when Great-Grandad was safely in bed, Mr Henning and Mr Durleston had a private, very private talk with Mr and Mrs Philpot together. The farmer and his wife listened, amazed. When they heard that Mr Henning proposed to hand them a cheque for £5,000 merely for the right to do a little digging, Mrs Philpot almost cried!

'And I have advised Mr Henning that he should offer you further sums, if he finds anything he would like to take back to the States with him, as – er – as mementos of a very pleasant stay here,' finished Mr Durleston.

'It sounds too good to be true,' said Mrs Philpot. 'We could certainly do with the money, couldn't we Trevor?'

Mr Henning took out his cheque book and produced his pen before Mr Philpot could say anything else. He wrote out the sum of £5,000, and signed the cheque with a flourish. He then presented it to Mr Philpot.

'And I hope there'll be more cheques to come,' he said. 'Thank you, sir. I'll get men along tomorrow to start digging.'

'I'll have a formal agreement drawn up,' put in Mr Durleston, thinking that he saw a rather doubtful look coming over Mr Philpot's face as he took the cheque. 'But you can cash the cheque straight away. Well, we'll leave you to talk it over!'

When the twins and the four heard of this the next morning, they were astounded. Mrs Philpot told the twins first, and Harry and Harriet ran at once to find the others. They listened, amazed and angry.

'How did they know all that? How did they guess where to find the castle site?' said Dick, fiercely. 'I bet it's that snoopy little Junior who put them on to this! I bet he spied on us! I *thought* I saw two people up on that hill after tea yesterday. It must have been Mr Henning and that friend of his – with Junior. Gosh, I could pull that kid's hair out!'

'Well, I suppose there's absolutely nothing we can do now!' said George, angrily. 'The next thing we'll see is lorries rolling up with men inside, and spades and drills and goodness knows what!'

She was quite right! That very morning the hill became quite a busy place! Four men had already been hired by Mr Henning, and they all went up the hill in their lorry, bumping slowly along, past the kitchen-midden mound, and on up to the shallow basin-like depression near the summit of the hill. Spades, forks and drills rattled in the lorry. Junior was mad with joy, and danced about at a safe distance, yelling defiance at the six children.

'You thought I didn't know anything, didn't you! I heard *everything*! Serves you right! Yah!'

'Timmy – chase him!' ordered George, in a furious voice. 'But don't hurt him, mind. Go on!'

And off went Timmy at a gallop, and if Junior hadn't leapt into the lorry and picked up a spade, Timmy would certainly have rolled him over and over on the ground!

Now what was to be done? The children almost gave up – but not quite! There *might* be something they could do – there might! *Why* was Julian suddenly looking so excited?

14   Snippet and Nosey are very helpful

'Listen!' said Julian, lowering his voice, and looking all about to make sure that no one was near. 'Do you remember what you told us, George, about a secret passage from the castle to the old chapel?'

'Yes! Yes! I do!' said George, and Anne nodded, her eyes bright. 'You mean the story that old Mr Finniston told us, down at the little antique shop, about the Lady of the castle taking her children in safety from the burning castle, by way of an underground passage to the old chapel? Gosh, I'd forgotten that!'

'Oh, Julian! Yes, George is right!' said Anne. 'Are you thinking that the passage might still be there, hidden underground?'

'What I think is this,' said Julian. 'If the Lady and her children escaped *underground*, they must first have fled down into the cellars of the castle – and so the passage or tunnel must have *started* from there. They couldn't have escaped in any other way because the castle was itself surrounded by enemies. So she must have gone with her children to hide in the cellars – and then, when the castle fell, she took them safely down the secret passage that led to the old chapel. So *that* means . . .'

'That means that if we can find the secret passage, we can get into the cellars ourselves – perhaps before the workmen do!' cried George, almost shouting with excitement.

'Exactly,' said Julian, his eyes shining. 'Now don't let's lose our heads and get too excited. Let's talk about it quietly – and for GOODNESS sake keep a watch for Junior.'

'Timmy – on guard!' said George, and Timmy at once went some paces away, and stood up straight, looking now in this direction, and now in that. Nobody could come within sight now, without Timmy giving a warning bark!

The children settled down beside a hedge. 'What's the plan?' asked Dick.

'I vote we go to the old chapel, take a line from there to the castle site, and walk slowly up that line,' said Julian. 'We might *possibly* see something that would guide us as to where the secret passage is. I don't know what – maybe the grass might be slightly different in colour – a bit darker than the surrounding grass, just as it was on the castle site. Anyway, it's worth trying. If we *do* see a line of darker grass, or something like that, we'll dig down underground ourselves, hoping the secret passage is underneath!'

'Oh *Ju*! What a wonderful idea!' said Anne. 'Come on, let's go down to the chapel straight away!'

So off they all went, Timmy, Snippet and Nosey the jackdaw too. He loved being with Snippet, though he teased him unmercifully. They arrived quickly at the chapel door and went in. 'I always feel as if there ought to be an organ playing when I'm inside,' said Anne, looking round the stacked sacks of grain.

'Never mind about organs,' said Julian, standing at the open door, and pointing up the hill. 'Now, see, there's the place where the old castle stood – where the men are already at work – and if we take a fairly

straight line to it, we *should* be more or less walking
over the old passage. I should think the men who made
it would drive as straight a tunnel as they could, to save
themselves work. A winding one would take a long
time.'

'I can't see that the grass is any different in colour,
along the line I'm looking,' said Dick, squinting, and
everyone agreed, very disappointed.

'So there's nothing to help us!' said George, mourn-
fully. 'All we can do is to work in a straight line up the
hill, and hope to find something that will tell us if
we're over a tunnel. Hollow-sounding footsteps,
perhaps!'

'That's very doubtful, I'm afraid,' said Julian. 'Still,
I can't see that we can do anything else. Come on,
then. All right, Tim, you can come back to us. Look at
Nosey, on Snippet's back again! That's right, Snippet,
roll over and get him off'

'Chack!' said Nosey, crossly, as he flew up in the air.
'Chack!'

The six children walked up the slope in as straight a
line as they could. They came right up to where the
men were digging, without having seen or heard
anything of any help at all. It was most disappointing.
Junior saw them, and yelled loudly.

'Children not allowed here! Keep off! My dad's
bought this place!'

'Liar!' shouted back the two Harries at once.
'You've got the right to dig and that's all!'

'Yah!' yelled Junior. 'You wait! Now don't you
set that great dog on me again! I'll tell my pop,
see?'

Timmy barked loudly, and Junior disappeared in a
hurry. George laughed. 'Silly little idiot! Why doesn't
somebody box his ears? I bet one of the men will

before he's many hours older. Look at him trying to use that drill!'

Junior was certainly not at all popular. He made himself a great nuisance, and in the end his father put him roughly into a lorry and told him to stay there. He howled dismally, but as no one paid any attention, he soon stopped!

The six children went slowly back down the gentle slope of the hill, taking a slightly different line, still hopeful. The jackdaw flew down to Harry's shoulder, chacking loudly, bored with all this walking! He suddenly saw Snippet sitting down to scratch his neck, and at once launched himself at him. He knew that the poodle always shut his eyes when he scratched himself, and that that was a very good time to give him a well-placed peck!

But, unfortunately for Nosey, the poodle opened his eyes too soon, and saw the jackdaw just about to perch on him! He snapped at him – and got him by the wing! 'Chack-chack-CHACK!' cried the jackdaw, urgently calling for help. 'CHACK!'

Harry ran to Snippet, shouting, 'Drop him, Snippet, drop him! You'll break his wing!' Before he could reach the pair, the jackdaw managed to free himself by giving Snippet a sudden peck on his nose, which made him bark in pain. As soon as he opened his mouth to bark, the jackdaw dropped on the ground, and scuttled away, his wing drooping, unable to fly.

The poodle was after him in a second! The twins yelled in vain. He meant to catch that exasperating jackdaw if it was the last thing he did! The squawking bird looked anxiously for a hiding place – and saw one! A rabbit hole – just the thing to hop down in a trice! In he went with another loud squawk, and disappeared from sight.

'He's gone down that rabbit hole!' said Dick, with a shout of laughter. 'Clever old bird. You're outwitted, Snippet!'

But no – Snippet wasn't! He disappeared down the hole too! He was as small as a rabbit, and could easily run down a burrow. He had never done more than sniff at one before, being rather scared of dark tunnels – but if Nosey had gone down, well, he would too!

The children stared in surprise. First the jackdaw – now Snippet! The twins bent down by the hole and yelled. 'Come back, Snippet, you idiot! The hill's honey combed with old warrens – you'll get lost for ever. Come back! Snippet. Snip-Snip-Snippet, can you hear us! COME HERE!'

There was silence down the rabbit-hole. No chack, no bark. 'They must have gone deep down,' said Harry, anxiously. 'There's a perfect maze of burrows in this hill. Dad said there used to be thousands of rabbits here at one time. Hey, Snippet – COME HERE!'

'Well, we'd better sit down till they come back,' said Anne, feeling suddenly tired with excitement and with climbing up hill and down.

'Right,' said Julian. 'Anyone got any sweets?'

'I have,' said George, as usual, and took out a rather grimy packet of peppermints. 'Here you are; have one, twins?'

'Thanks,' they said. 'We really ought to be getting back – we've plenty of work to do!'

They sat sucking their peppermints, wondering what in the world the jackdaw and Snippet were up to. At last Timmy pricked up his ears and gave a small bark, looking at the entrance of the burrow as he did so. 'They're coming,' said George. 'Timmy knows!'

Sure enough, Timmy was right. Out came first Snippet, and then Nosey, apparently quite good friends again. Snippet rushed to the twins and flung himself on them as if he hadn't seen them for days. He put something down at their feet. 'What's this you've found?' said Harry, picking it up. 'Some dirty old bone?'

Julian suddenly took it from him, almost snatching it. 'Bone? No – that's not a bone. It's a small carved dagger with a broken handle – old as the hills! SNIPPET! Where did you find it?'

'The jackdaw's got something too!' cried Anne, pointing to him. 'Look – in his beak!'

Harriet caught the jackdaw easily, for he still could not fly. 'It's a ring!' she said. 'With a red stone in it – look!'

All six children gazed at the two strange articles. An old carved knife, black with age – and an old ring, with a stone still set in it! They could have come from only one place! George said what everyone was thinking.

'Snippet and the jackdaw have been to the cellars of the castle! They must have! That burrow must have led *straight* into the tunnel that goes to the dungeons and the cellars – and they've been there! Oh, Snippet – you clever, clever dog – you've told us JUST what we want to know!'

'George is right!' said Dick, jubilantly. 'We know quite a lot of things now, because of Snippet and Nosey. We know there must be plenty of things still in those castle cellars – and we know that *some*where near the end of this burrow is the secret passage – because that's the only way they could have got into the cellars – by using the passage! The burrow led into the passage! Don't you agree, Julian?'

'You bet!' said Julian, flushed with excitement. 'My word, this *is* a bit of good luck! Hurray for Snippet and Nosey. Look, the jackdaw's trying to fly, his wing isn't badly hurt – just bruised, I expect. Good old Nosey – little did he know what his bit of mischief would lead to!'

'What happens now?' said George, her eyes shining. 'Do *we* dig, too – now that we know where the passage is? It can't be very far; and once we've got down to it, we can easily get into the cellars – before that American does!'

WHAT an excitement! Timmy really thought everyone had gone completely mad!

15 Digging for the secret tunnel

'How can we get permission to dig?' asked Anne. 'I mean – will we be allowed to?'

'I don't see why not – Mr Henning has only been given permission to dig in one place,' said Julian. 'I bet we'd get permission to dig just here – it's a pretty good way from the castle site, anyway.'

'Why shouldn't we just dig and see if anyone stops us?' said George. 'If Mr Philpot stops us, we could tell him what we're *really* doing. He'd probably let us, then. But whatever happens, we don't want *Mr Henning* to know what we've discovered – or *think* we've discovered!'

'Well, what shall we say then, if he asks why we're digging?' said Anne.

'Say silly things – joke about it!' said Dick. 'Twins, have you work to do this morning? Can you find us spades, do you think?'

'Yes – you can have our spades, and Dad's old ones, too!' said Harry. 'We wish we could help – but we've tons to do, and we're very late already.'

'Oh dear – and I promised that George and I would help in the kitchen!' said Anne. 'And pick peas for dinner and pod them – and get more raspberries! Can you and Dick dig all on your own, Ju?'

'Good heavens, yes!' said Julian. 'It'll be slower with just two of us digging, but we'll soon get deep down, you'll see! Anyway, we could all take turns this afternoon, perhaps, if the twins finish their work.'

'We will! We'll do it at top speed!' said Harry and Harriet together. 'Now we'll get some spades for you.'

They raced off, with Snippet beside them, and the two girls went down the hill more slowly, feeling very thrilled. If only, only they could dig down and find the secret passage from the chapel to the cellars of the old castle! Timmy felt the excitement and wagged his tail happily. He was always happy when George was thrilled about anything.

Harriet soon brought two big spades and two smaller ones to the boys. They were heavy, and she panted as she carried them up the hill.

'Good girl – or is it good boy?' asked Dick, as he took the spades. 'Wait – it's Harriet, isn't it? You've no scar on your hand!'

Harriet grinned and ran off swiftly to join her brother in the farm work that was their task. Julian gazed after her. 'They're good kids,' he said, as he turned to drive his spade into the earth. 'Worth a hundred Juniors! Funny how some children are made of such good stuff, and others aren't worth a penny. Well, Dick – go to it! This earth is pretty hard. I wish we could borrow one of those machines the men are using up there!'

They dug hard, and were soon very hot indeed. They stripped themselves to their shorts, but were still far too hot. They greeted Anne with joy when she laboured up the slope, carrying a jug of cool lemonade and some buns.

'I say! You've made quite a hole already!' she said. 'How far down do you think the tunnel will be?'

'Well, not too far down, really,' said Dick, taking a long drink of the lemonade. 'This is super, Anne.

Thanks a lot. We've dug into the burrow, and we're following it at the moment – hoping it will enter the secret tunnel before we're too tired to dig any more!'

'I say – here comes Junior!' said Anne suddenly, looking up the slope. Sure enough, it was the American boy, feeling quite brave now that neither Timmy nor Snippet was about.

He stopped a little way away and shouted: 'What do you think you're doing, digging in our hill?'

'Go away and lose yourself!' shouted back Dick. 'This isn't your hill! If you can dig, so can we!'

'Copy-cats!' shouted Junior. 'My pop's laughing his head off about you!'

'Well, tell him to pick it up before it rolls down the hill!' yelled Dick. 'Clear off!'

Junior watched them for a little while, puzzled, and then went off up the hill, presumably to report to his father. Anne laughed and went back to the farmhouse.

'As his pop doesn't know a thing about the secret passage, he must think we're off our heads, digging here,' said Julian, with a chuckle. 'Well, let him think so. He'll be off *his* head with rage when he finds out what we're really doing – and he won't know that till we're in the cellars!'

Dick laughed, and wiped his forehead again. 'I wish this burrow would come to an end. And I hope to goodness it *does* lead into the side of the tunnel. I don't want to have to dig up half the hillside. The ground's so hard and dry.'

'Well, thank goodness it's getting sandy here,' said Julian, driving his spade deeper down. He suddenly gave a cry. 'I say! My spade went right down by itself, then! I believe I've come to the secret passage! The burrow must go right through one side of it!'

He was right! The rabbit hole ran sideways and

down – and into a passage! The boys dug feverishly now, panting, their hair falling over their foreheads, perspiration dripping off their faces.

Soon they had a deep hole, fairly wide – and at the bottom of it a way into the tunnel beneath! They lay down and peered into it. 'It's just over a metre below the surface,' said Dick. 'We might have had to do much more digging than this! Whew, I'm hot!'

'It must be dinner-time,' said Julian. 'I don't really like to leave our hole, now that we've got down to the tunnel. And yet we simply MUST have something to eat. I'm ravenous!'

'So am I. But if we leave the hole unguarded, that pest of a Junior might come along and climb down and find the passage!' said Dick. 'Look – here comes George – with old Tim. I wonder if she'd leave him here to guard the hole.'

George was delighted to hear their news. She gazed down the hole in great excitement. 'How deeply you've dug!' she said. 'No wonder you're hot. My word – if Mr Henning knew what you've found, he'd be down here in two shakes of a duck's tail!'

'He certainly would,' said Julian, soberly. 'That's what we're afraid of. Or that snoopy Junior might climb down into the hole, if he came along. He's been here already to see what we're doing.'

'We're scared of going in to dinner, in case one of them comes along and investigates the hole while it's unguarded,' said Dick. 'And we wondered if . . .'

But George interrupted him, almost as if she knew what he was going to say. 'I'll leave Timmy here on guard, while you come down to dinner,' she said. 'He won't let anyone come within metres of it!'

'Thanks, old thing,' said the boys gratefully, and went off down the hill with George, leaving Timmy behind. 'On guard, Timmy,' said George. 'On guard. Don't let *anyone* come near that hole.'

'Woof,' said Timmy, understanding at once, and looking fiercely all round and about him. He lay down with a small growl. Let anyone come near the boys' hole, if they dare!

They did dare – but when they saw Timmy leaping to his feet, the hackles on his neck thick and upright, and heard his deep, continuous growl, Junior and his father thought better of it, and went on down the hill to have dinner at the farmhouse. Poor Mr Durleston trailed behind them, almost knocked out by the heat of the sun.

'Silly kids,' said Mr Henning to Junior. 'Thinking it's clever to dig just because *we're* digging? What do they suppose they'll find down there? Another kitchen-midden?'

Junior sent a stone scudding along towards Timmy – and then fled for his life as the dog came bounding angrily down the slope. Even Mr Henning hurried. He didn't like Timmy either!

That afternoon the twins, Julian, Dick, George, Anne and Snippet all climbed the hill to the hole, where Tim still lay watching for intruders. They brought him two fine bones, and a jug of water. He was very pleased indeed. Snippet danced round, hoping for a bite at a bone, and the jackdaw, his wing apparently quite recovered now, dared to go and peck at the bigger bone, even though Timmy growled warningly!

The twins were thrilled to see the deep hole. 'Can't we go down now? they said eagerly, both together.

'Yes – it would be a jolly good time to let ourselves slide into the tunnel,' said Julian. 'All the men working on the castle site have gone off to have dinner at the little village pub, and haven't yet come back – and the Hennings and Mr Durleston are safely at the farmhouse.'

'I'll go first,' said Dick, and lowered himself into the hole. He held on to the grassy edges and poked hard with his feet, to widen the opening into the tunnel. Then he let himself slide down until his legs were out of the rabbit hole, and dangled through the wall of the tunnel.

'Here we go!' he said, and let himself drop. Whooooosh! He slid right into a dark, musty tunnel, and landed on soft earth. 'Chuck me down a torch,' he shouted. 'It's pitch-dark in here. Did you remember to bring our torches, George?'

Yes, George had four! 'Look out!' she said. 'Here comes one!' And she dropped it down the hole. She had already switched it on, so Dick saw it coming and caught it neatly. He shone it into the dark place around him.

'Yes! It *is* a tunnel!' he shouted. 'The secret passage, no doubt about it! I say – isn't this great? Come on down, all of you, let's share in the find together. Let's walk right up to the castle cellars. Come on, everybody! Come on!'

16 Up the tunnel and into the cellars

Dick held up his torch to the hole, so that the others might see their way. One by one they slid into the dark tunnel, too excited for words. Timmy came too, and so did Snippet, but the jackdaw thought better of it, and remained at the enlarged opening of the burrow, chacking loudly.

The children swung their torches to and fro. 'That must be the way down to the old chapel,' said Julian, his torch shining down the dark tunnel. No one could stand upright just there except Timmy, for the roof was low. He sniffed suspiciously here and there, and kept close to George.

'Well – come on!' said Julian, his voice shaking a little with excitement. 'We'll go straight up, and see where the passage ends. My word – I can hardly wait to see what's at the top!'

They made their way slowly up the passage. There had been roof-falls here and there, but not enough to matter. Tree roots, withered and twining, sometimes caught their feet. 'Funny!' said Harry, in astonishment. 'There aren't any trees growing on the hillside here – why the roots, then?'

'They may be the remains of the roots of long-ago trees that did once grow on the hill,' said Julian, shining his torch up the passage, hoping against hope that there would be no serious obstacle to their journey. 'Hallo – what's this at my feet? *Two feathers!* Now how in the world did *they* get here!'

It was a puzzle! The children examined them earnestly by the light of their torches. Feathers – looking quite new too – how *did* they get there? Was there any other way into the passage – and had the birds found it?

Dick gave a shout of laughter that made everyone jump. 'We're idiots! They're two of the *jackdaw's* feathers – they must have dropped out of his bitten wing when he went down the burrow and up this passage with Snippet after him!'

'Of *course*! Why on earth didn't I think of that?' said Julian. They went on upwards once more, and then Julian suddenly stopped again. A curious humming noise had come down the dark, low tunnel, a throbbing that seemed to get right inside their heads.

'What's that?' said Anne, in great alarm. 'I don't like it.'

They all stood there, and felt, like Anne, that the noise was indeed inside their heads. They shook them, put their fingers into their ears – but it was no good. The strange throbbing went on and on.

'This is a bit too mysterious for me,' said Anne, scared. 'I don't think I want to go on.'

The noise stopped, and they all felt better at once – but almost immediately it started again. To everyone's surprise, George began to laugh.

'It's all right! It's only those men at work on the castle site. It's their drills we can hear – throbbing through the hillside, and down this passage right into our ears. They must be back from lunch. Cheer up, everybody!'

They all smiled in relief, though Anne's hands were still shaking a little as she held up her torch to shine through the black darkness. 'There's not an awful lot of air here,' she said. 'I hope we soon get into the cellars!'

'They can't be far,' said Julian. 'This tunnel goes in a pretty straight line, just as we thought it would. Where it curves, it's probable that the men of long ago who made it were forced to burrow round tree roots that blocked their way. Anyway, as we can hear the drills so loudly now, we can't be far from the castle site.'

They were nearer than they thought! Julian's torch suddenly shone on the remains of a great door, lying on the ground before him – the door that once shut off the cellars from the passage! The tunnel ceased just there, and the torches shone on a vast underground place, silent, full of shadows.

'We're there!' said Julian, in a whisper that went scurrying round in the darkness and came back as a strange echo that said: 'There-there-there-there-there.'

'That fallen door must have been one made all those years gone by!' said Anne, in awe. She touched a corner of it with her foot, and the wood crumbled into dust with a strange little sigh.

Snippet pushed in front of them and ran into the cellars. He gave a short bark as if to say, 'Come on – don't be afraid. *I've* been here before.'

'Oh, Snippet, be careful!' said Anne, half-afraid that everything would crumble away at the sound of Snippet's pattering feet!

'Let's go on – but carefully,' said Julian. 'Everything will be ready to crumble into dust – unless it's made of metal! It's a marvel that door was preserved like that – it looks good enough – but I'm sure if any of us sneezed it would be gone.'

'Don't make me laugh, please, Ju,' said Dick, stepping carefully round the fallen door. 'Even a laugh might do damage down here!'

Soon they were all in the blackness of the underground cellars. They flashed their torches around. 'What a vast place!' said Julian. 'Can't see any dungeons, though!'

'Thank goodness!' said Harriet and Anne together. They had both dreaded coming across old bones of long-forgotten prisoners!

'Look – there's an archway,' said George, shining her torch to the right. 'A fine, semicircular arch it is, too, made of stone – and there's another, look. They must lead into a main underground chamber, I should think. There's nothing much to see just here, except heaps of dirt. It all smells so musty, too!'

'Well, follow me carefully,' said Julian, and led the way towards the stone archways, his torch shining brightly. They came to one of the beautiful rounded arches and stood there, all four torches shining brightly into a large underground room.

'No cellars here – but just one great underground storeroom,' said Julian. 'The roof was shored up with great beams – see, some of them have fallen. And those stone arches must have borne much of the weight, too. Not one of those has fallen! They must have stood there for centuries – what wonderful workmanship!'

Dick and the twins were more interested in the great mass of jumble scattered about round the walls. It was covered with dust that rose lightly into the air when Timmy brushed against anything. Snippet ran round happily, sniffing everywhere, and sneezing every now and again as the fine dust went up his nose.

'Any treasures, do you think?' whispered Anne, and the echo came back weirdly, whispering too.

'Whispers seem to echo back more than our

ordinary voices!' said Julian. 'Hallo – what's this?'

They shone their torches on to the floor where lay what looked like a heap of blackened metal. Julian bent down and then gave a loud exclamation. 'Do you see what this is? A suit of armour! Almost perfect still. Look, though, it must be ages old – and here's another – and another! Were they old ones, thrown out – or spare ones? Look at this helmet – *grand*!'

He kicked it gently with his foot, and it gave out a metallic sound and rolled away a little. 'Would that be valuable now?' asked Harry, anxiously.

'Valuable! Worth its weight in gold, I should think!' said Julian, such excitement in his voice that everyone felt even more thrilled. Harriet called to him urgently.

'Julian – here's a chest of some sort. Quick!'

They went slowly over to where she stood, for they had already learnt that any quick movement raised clouds of fine, choking dust. She pointed to a great dark chest, its corners bound with iron, and with iron strapping all round it.

It was made of wood, as black with age as the iron itself. 'What's inside, do you think?' whispered Harriet, and at once her whisper echoed from every corner: 'You think, you think, you think . . .'

Timmy went to sniff at the chest – and to his amazement it disintegrated at once! Slowly, softly, the sides and the great lid fell into dust that settled gently on the ground around. Only the iron corners and strapping were left. It was strange to watch something crumble away before their eyes. Like magic! thought Anne.

As the wooden sides of the chest crumbled, something shone out brightly in the light of the torches – something that moved and slid out of the chest, as the sides fell away – fell with a jingling, clinking, sound, curious to hear in that silent darkness.

The children stared in astonishment, hardly believing their eyes. Anne clutched Julian and made him jump. 'Ju! What is it? Is it gold?'

Julian bent to pick up one of the rolling pieces. 'Yes! It's *gold*. No doubt about it. Gold never tarnishes, it keeps bright for ever. These are gold coins of some sort, treasured and hidden away. There couldn't have been time to take them, when the Lady fled with her children – and no one else would be able to get them, for the castle was burnt down and buried by the falling walls! This hoard of gold must have lain here untouched all these long years.'

'Waiting for *us* to come!' said George. 'Twins – your mother and father needn't worry about their farm any more! With the proceeds from the treasures down here they will be able to buy all the tractors and equipment they could possibly need! Julian, there's another chest, look – like this one, but smaller, and beginning to fall to pieces. Let's see what's inside that! More gold, I hope.'

But the second chest did not hold gold pieces – it held a different kind of treasure! One side had burst open, and its contents had dribbled out.

'Rings!' said Anne, picking up two from the dust in which they lay.

'A golden belt!' said George. 'And look – these tarnished chains must be necklaces, because they're set with blue stones. This must be where the jackdaw found that ring!'

'*We've* found something else, too!' called Harry, his excited voice making everyone jump. 'Look – racks of swords and daggers! Some are beautifully carved, too!'

Clamped to the wall were iron racks, held in place

by great iron rods driven deep into the hard earth of the wall. Some had loosened and the racks hung crooked, their knives and swords askew, or lay on the floor. Snippet ran to pick one up – just as he had done before when he and Nosey first went into the cellars by themselves!

'What wonderful swords!' said Julian, picking one up. 'My word, this one's heavy! I can hardly hold it! Good gracious – what's that?'

Something had fallen from the roof of the cellar in which they were standing – a great piece of old wood, that had originally been placed there as part of the roofing. At the same time the continual hum of the drilling above rose to a roar that made the children jump.

Julian gave a shout. 'Out of here, quickly!' he yelled. 'Those men will soon be through the roof, and it may suddenly fall and bury us! We'll have to go at once!'

He snatched a dagger from the rack, and, still with the sword in his hand, ran back to the entrance of the secret passage, pulling Anne with him. The twins were last of all, for they had run to get a handful of the gold, and two of the necklaces and rings. They *must* show their mother a few of the treasures, they must!

Just as they reached the entrance, more of the roof fell. 'We'll have to stop this excavating,' panted Julian, looking back. 'If the roof falls in, it may destroy many of the old treasures there!'

They hurried into the dark, low tunnel, feeling more excited than they had ever felt in their lives! Timmy led the way, glad to think they were going out into the open air once more!

'What will Mother say?' the twins kept saying to one another. 'WhatEVER will she say!'

17 Trapped!

The six children stumbled down the tunnel, still hearing the far-off sound of the drills, and fearing that at any moment the cellars would be discovered by Mr Henning, who, no doubt, would be anxiously watching from above!

They came to where they thought the burrow must be, that Dick had dug through – but instead, there was nothing but a great mass of earth, some of it seeping into the tunnel! Julian gazed at it by the light of his torch, dismayed.

'The burrow's fallen in!' he said, his voice shaking. 'What are we to do?' We've no spades to dig ourselves out!'

'We can use our hands,' said Dick, and began to scrabble at the fallen earth, sweeping it into the tunnel. But as he scrabbled, more and more earth fell into the widened burrow, and Julian stopped Dick at once. 'No more of that, Dick – you might start an earthfall, and we'd all be buried alive. Oh gosh – this is awful! We'll have to go back up the passage and try to make the men hear us shouting, BLOW! That means Mr Henning will know what we're up to.'

'I don't believe the men will be there much longer,' said Dick, looking at his watch. 'They pack up at five, and it's almost that now. My word, we've been ages – Mrs Philpot will wonder where we all are.'

'The drilling has just stopped,' said Anne. 'I haven't

got that awful noise inside my ears any longer.'

'In that case, it's certainly no good going back up the tunnel,' said Julian. 'They'd be gone before we got there. I say, you know – this is serious. I ought to have thought of this – any idiot knows that ground entrances to passages should be strengthened, if they're newly dug!'

'Well, we can always go back to the cellars and wait for the men to come tomorrow,' said George, sounding more cheerful than she felt.

'How do we know they'll be there tomorrow?' said Dick. 'Henning may have paid them off today, if he's disappointed in his hopes!'

'Don't be such a dismal Jimmy!' said George, sensing that the twins were getting panicky. They certainly *were* worried – but more because they were certain that their mother would be scared to death if they didn't come home, than for their own safety.

Timmy had been standing patiently beside George, waiting to get out of the hole. At last, tired of waiting, he trotted away – but *down* the tunnel – not up!

'Timmy! Where are you going?' cried George, and shone her torch on him. He turned his head and looked at her, showing quite clearly by his manner that he was tired of standing about, and intended to find out where the tunnel led!

'Ju, look at Timmy! He wants us to go *down* the tunnel!' cried George. 'Why didn't we think of that?'

'I don't know! I'm afraid I thought it would be a sort of blind alley!' said Julian. 'I fear it will, too. Nobody knows where the chapel entrance to the tunnel is, do they, twins?'

'No,' they said, both together. 'It's never been discovered, as far as *we* know.'

'Anyway, it's worth trying,' said George, her voice

sounding muffled as she went down the passage after the impatient Timmy. 'I'm getting suffocated in here!'

The others followed, Snippet dancing along behind, thinking the whole thing was a huge joke. The tunnel, as the children had imagined, went downwards in more or less a straight line. It had fallen in slightly here and there, but by bending their heads and crouching low, they managed to get through. Finally they came to a bad fall of earth from the roof, and had to crawl through on hands and knees. Anne didn't like that part at all!

They came at last into a strange little place, where the tunnel ended abruptly. It was like a stone vault – a little chamber about one and a half metres high and two metres square. Julian looked up fearfully at its low roof. Was it of stone? If so, they were trapped. They would never be able to lift a heavy stone slab!

No – not all the roof was made of stone. A piece in the middle about a metre square was made of strong stout wood, which rested on ledges cut in the stone.

'It looks like a trap-door,' said Julian, examining it by the light of his torch. 'I wonder if we are just below the floor of the old chapel? Dick, if you and I and Harry all heave at the same time, we might be able to move this trap-door.'

So they all heaved, George, too – but although the door did lift a little at one corner, it simply could *not* be moved upwards.

'I know why we can't move it,' said Harry, red in the face with heaving. 'There are sacks of grain and fertiliser and all kinds of stuff spread over the floor of the old chapel! They're heavy as lead! We'd never be able to move that trap-door if two or three sacks are on it!'

'Gosh – I didn't think of that,' said Julian, his heart

sinking. 'Didn't you know of this entrance into the tunnel, twins?'

'Of course not!' said Harry. 'Nobody did. I can't think why it wasn't known, though. Except, of course, that a storehouse like this has its floor always covered with sacks of something, and with the spillings out of those sacks! It may not have been cleaned out or swept for hundreds of years!'

'Well, what are we to do now?' demanded Dick. 'We can't stay here in this stuffy little place!'

'Listen – I can hear something!' said George suddenly. 'Noises overhead.'

They listened intently, and, through the tightly fitting oak trap-door above them, they heard a loud voice shouting. 'GIVE US A HAND, BILL WILL YOU?'

'It's Jamie – the men are working overtime this week!' said Harry. 'He's come to get something out of the chapel. Quick, let's all yell and hammer on the trap-door with whatever we've got that'll make a noise!'

At once there was a riot of sound from the little vault – yells, shouts, barks, and the hammering of sword handles and fists on the wooden slab overhead. Then the children ceased their hammering, and fell silent, listening. They heard Jamie's voice, lifted in wonder.

'Bill! What in the name of goodness was that? A rat-fight, do you suppose?'

'They heard us,' said Julian, excited. 'Come on – once again. And bark the place down, Timmy!'

Timmy was only too ready to oblige, for he was very tired of tunnels and dark, echoing places by now! He barked long and fiercely, frightening Snippet so much that the little poodle actually ran back up the tunnel! What with Tim's barking, and everyone's yelling, and the constant hammering, the noise was even louder than before, and Bill and Jamie listened in amazement.

'Comes from over there,' said Bill. Something's going on there. Beats me what it is though. If it were night-time, I'd think it were ghosties having a game! Come on – we'll have a look.'

The place was so full of sacks that the two men had to clamber over the rows, disturbing the cat and her kittens. She had curled herself round them, scared of the unexpected noise.

'This corner, Bill,' said Jamie, standing on top of two layers of sacks. He put his hands to his mouth and bellowed like a bull.

'ANYONE ABOUT?'

The six below answered frantically at the tops of their voices, Timmy barking too.

'There's a dog barking down there,' said Bill, scratching his head, puzzled, looking down at the sacks as if he thought there might be a dog in one of them.

'A dog! There're folks as well,' said Jamie, astounded. 'Where are they? Can't be under these sacks!'

'Maybe they're in that little old store place we found one day, in the floor,' suggested Bill. 'Remember? Under an old trap-door, it were, that were covered by a great slab of stone. You remember, man!'

'Oh ay,' said Jamie, and then the clamour began again, for the children were now getting near despair. 'Come on, Bill,' said Jamie, hearing the note of urgency, though he couldn't make out a word from below. 'Heave over these here sacks. We've got to get to the bottom of this!'

They heaved a dozen sacks away, and then at last the trap-door was uncovered. The stone slab that had once hidden it had been taken up some years ago by the two men and now stood against the wall. They had not bothered to replace it, not guessing that the 'little old store place' as they had thought it, was really an entrance to a secret, long-forgotten passage. It was fortunate indeed for the children that only the old wooden trap-door was between them and the men, for if the stone slab had been there too, no sound of their shouting would have been heard in the old chapel above!

'Now for this here trap-door,' said Bill. He tapped on it with his great boot. 'Who's down here?' he demanded, wondering what the answer would be.

'US!' shrieked the twins, and the others joined in, with Timmy barking frantically again.

'Bless us all – that's the twins' voices I heard!' said Jamie. 'How did they climb into the storeroom without moving these here sacks?'

With a great heave the two men pulled up the heavy wooden slab, and looked down in the greatest astonishment at the little crowd below! They couldn't believe their eyes! Timmy was the first out. He leapt upwards and landed beside the men, wagging his great tail and licking them lavishly.

'Oh, thanks, Bill, thanks, Jamie,' cried the twins as the two men pulled them up. 'Gosh, I'm thankful you were working overtime – and happened to come in here!'

'Your ma's been hollering for you,' said Bill, disapprovingly. 'And didn't you say you were going to help me with those poles?'

'How did you get down there?' demanded Jamie, pulling up the others one by one. Julian was the last, and he handed up poor scared little Snippet, who really felt he had had quite enough adventures for one day!

'Oh – it's too long a story to tell you just now,' said

Harry. 'But thanks again most awfully, Bill and Jamie. Can you put that slab back? Don't tell anyone we were down there till we tell you how it happened, see? Now we'll have to rush and tell Mother we're all right!'

And away they all went, longing for tea, tired out, full of thankfulness at their escape from the little stone room under the chapel floor. What *would* everyone say when they displayed the treasures they had brought back with them?

18   A great story to tell!

The twins tore down to the farmhouse, and saw their mother still looking for them. They flung themselves on her, and she gave them a loving shake.

'Where have you been? You're an hour late for tea, all of you. I've been so worried. Mr Henning told me some story about you digging up on the hillside!'

'Mother! We're ravenous, so let's have tea and we'll tell you some great news,' said the twins, both together. 'Mother, you *will* be astonished. Where's Dad – and Great-Grandad too?'

'They're still at the tea-table – they were late too,' said Mrs Philpot. 'They've been out looking for you all! Great-Grandad isn't very pleased. What in the world have you brought with you? Surely those are not *swords*?'

'Mother, let's have tea first and we'll tell you EVERY-THING!' said the twins. '*Must* we wash? Oh blow – all right, come on, everyone, let's wash. And we'll put our treasures down in the darkest corner, so that Dad and Great-Grandad won't see them till we're ready to show them!'

Soon they were all sitting down at the tea-table, glad to see a wonderful spread! Great slices of thickly buttered bread, home-made jam, home-made cheese, a fat ginger cake, a fruit cake, a dish of ripe plums, and even a home-cooked ham if anyone wanted something more substantial!

Mr Philpot and old Great-Grandad were still at the table, drinking a last cup of tea. Mrs Philpot had told them that the children had to wash, but would tell all that had happened when they came to their tea.

'Hoo!' said Great-Grandad, frowning till his great bushy eyebrows almost covered his nose. 'When I was a boy I daren't come in one minute late for my meals! You twins have worried your mother – that's bad!'

'We're awfully sorry, Great-Grandad,' said the twins, in unison. 'But just wait till you hear our story. Julian – you tell it!'

And so, between great munches of bread and butter, ham sandwiches, and slices of cake, the story was told, all the children joining in now and again.

Great-Grandad already knew that Mr Henning had been given permission to excavate, and that a cheque for £5,000 had been given to Mr Philpot. He had flown into a terrible temper, and only when Mrs Philpot had sobbed and said that she would give it back, though she could hardly bear to part with it, had Great-Grandad given in. Now ready to fly into another rage, he listened to the children's story. He forgot to drink his cooling tea. He forgot to fill his pipe. He even forgot to ask a single question! Never had he heard such a wonderful, glorious tale in his life!

Julian told the story well, and the others filled in any bits he left out. Mrs Philpot's eyes almost fell out of her head when she heard how Snippet and Nosey had gone into the rabbit burrow and come out with a broken dagger and a ring!

'But – but where did . . .' she began, and listened again, to hear how Dick and Julian had enlarged the burrow, crawled right through it, and slid down into the long-lost secret tunnel!

'HA!' said Great-Grandad, getting out his great red

handkerchief, and dabbing his forehead with it. 'HA! Wish I'd been there. Go on, go on!'

Julian had stopped to drink his tea. He laughed and went on, describing how they had all gone up the tunnel with their torches, the dogs with them.

'It was dark and smelly, and suddenly we heard a terrific noise!' he said.

'It got right inside our heads!' put in Anne.

'What was it, what was it?' said Great-Grandad, his eyes almost as big as the saucer in front of him.

'The noise of the men drilling up on the old castle site,' said Julian, and Great-Grandad exploded in wrath. He pointed his pipe at his grandson, the farmer. 'Didn't I tèll you I wouldn't have those men on my farm?' he began, and then calmed down as Mrs Philpot patted his arm, shushing him. 'Go on, Julian,' she said.

And then came the really exciting part, the story of how they came into the actual cellars of the castle – the stone archways – the age-old dust . . .

'And the echoes!' said Anne. 'When we whispered, a hundred other whispers came back!'

When Julian described their finds – the old armour, still good, but black with age – the rack of swords and knives and daggers – the chest of gold . . .

'GOLD! I don't believe you!' shouted Great-Grandad. 'You're making that up, young man. Don't you pile up your tale too much, now. Stick to the truth.'

The twins promptly took some of the gold coins out of their pockets, still brilliant and shining. They laid them on the table in front of the three amazed grown-ups.

'There you are! *They* will tell you if we are making up all this or not – these gold coins! They will speak more loudly than words!'

In awe Mr Philpot picked them up, and passed them

one by one to the old man, and to his wife. Great-
Grandad was dumbfounded and dumbstruck. He
simply could not say a single word. He could only
grunt and puff as he turned the coins over in his great
horny hand.

'Are they really gold?' said Mrs Philpot, quite over-
come at the sudden appearance of the shining coins.
'Trevor – will they belong to *us*? Does it mean – does it
mean that we'll be well enough off to buy a new
tractor for you – and . . .'

'Depends how much of this stuff there is, up in those
old cellars,' said Mr Philpot, trying to keep calm. 'And
depends on how much we're allowed to keep, of
course. Might belong to the Crown by now.'

'THE CROWN!' roared Great-Grandad, standing up
suddenly. 'The CROWN!' No, SIR! It's mine! Ours!
Found on my land, put there by our ancestors. Yes –
and I'll give old Mr Finniston down in the village a
share, so I will. He's been a good friend of mine for
years!'

The children thought that was quite a good idea!
They then showed the jewellery they had brought,
and Mrs Philpot marvelled at it, tarnished though it
was.

But the swords and dagger brought the greatest
excitement to old Great-Grandad and his grandson,
Mr Philpot! As soon as they heard that the children had
actually brought back some of the old weapons, the
two men got up and went to get them. Great-Grandad
picked up the biggest and heaviest of the swords, and
swung it dangerously round his head, looking like a
reincarnation of some fearsome old warrior, with his
great beard and blazing eyes.

'No, no Grandad!' said Mrs Philpot in fright. 'Oh,
you'll knock down the things on the dresser – there, I

knew you would! Bang goes my meat dish!'

And down it went, CRASH! Timmy and Snippet almost jumped out of their skins, and began to bark frantically.

'Sit DOWN, all of you!' cried Mrs Philpot to the excited dogs and the men. 'Let Julian finish his story! Great-Grandad, SIT DOWN!'

'Ha,' said Great-Grandad, a broad smile on his face, sitting down in his chair. 'HA! Did me good to swing that sword. Where's that American? I might try it out on him!'

The children roared with delight. It was great to see the old man so delighted. 'Go on with that tale of yours,' he said to Julian. 'You tell it well, boy. Go on! Now, Ma, don't you take my sword away. I'm keeping it here, between my legs, in case I want to use it. HA!'

Julian quickly finished his tale, and told how they had walked back down the passage and found their burrow entrance fallen in – and then gone right down the rest of the tunnel and come at last into the little stone-walled room.

'And we couldn't get out,' said Julian. 'There was a great wooden trap-door over our heads, and on it lay a dozen or so sacks – heavy as lead! We couldn't lift it. So we yelled!'

'So *that's* where the secret passage led to!' said Mr Philpot. 'How did you get out?'

'We yelled and hammered, and Bill and Jamie heard us, and pulled off the sacks, and lifted up the old trapdoor,' said Julian. 'Gosh, we were glad to see them! We thought we might be lost for ever! Jamie knew about the little stone vault down under the chapel floor – but he thought it was just an old storeroom!'

'I've never heard of it before,' said Mrs Philpot, and old Great-Grandad nodded his head in agreement.

'No more have I,' he said. 'For as long as I can remember the floor of that old chapel has been piled with sacks, and what bits I could see of the floor were covered with thick dust. Yes, even when I was a boy, playing hide and seek in the old place, it was full of sacks – and that's every bit of eighty-five years ago now! Well, well – seems like yesterday I was playing in there with a cat and her kittens!'

·'There's a cat and her kittens there now,' said Anne.

'Ay, little lass – and there'll be a cat and her kittens there when you're an old, old woman!' said Great-Grandad. 'There's some things never change, thanks be to the Lord. Well, well – I can sleep easy of a night now – I reckon you and the farm will be all right Trevor, with the money you'll make out of those old finds – and I'll live to see the twins growing up and handling the finest farm in Dorset, so I shall – with everything newfangled they want, bless their bonny faces! And now I'll just have one more swing with that sword!'

The children fled! Great-Grandad looked years younger already – and goodness knows *what* damage he would do with that great sword! What an afternoon it had been – one they would never forget!

19 'The most exciting adventure we've ever had!'

After all the excitement of the afternoon the children felt lazy. The twins went off to feed the chickens. 'Better late than never!' they said, together.

'Where are Mr Henning and Mr Durleston and that awful Junior, Mrs Philpot?' asked George, getting up to help with the washing of the tea things.

'Oh, Mr Henning came in to say he and Mr Durleston were going to a meal at a hotel, and taking Junior too,' said Mrs Philpot. 'He seemed very pleased with himself indeed. He said that they had broken through to the cellars of the old castle, and expected great things – and that maybe a second cheque of £5,000 would be coming soon!'

'You won't take it, though, will you, Mrs Philpot?' said Julian quickly, overhearing what was being said. 'The things down in that cellar will be worth much more than any money Mr Henning is likely to offer you. He'd only take them to America and sell them for vast sums and make a huge profit. Why should you let him do that?'

'That nice old man, Mr Finniston, down in the little antique shop, would know what everything was worth,' said George. 'And he's a descendant of the long-ago Finnistons of Finniston Castle, isn't he – he'll be thrilled to bits when he hears what's been happening!'

'We'll send word for him to come up tomorrow,' decided Mrs Philpot. 'After all, Mr Henning has *his* adviser – that surly Mr Durleston. We'll have Mr Finniston for ours. Great-Grandad would be pleased about that – they're great friends, those two.'

There was however, no need to send for Mr Finniston, for Great-Grandad had himself gone down straight away to tell the great news to his old crony. What a talk they had together!

'Gold coins – jewellery – suits of armour – swords – and goodness knows what else!' said Great-Grandad for the twentieth time, and old Mr Finniston listened gravely, nodding his head. 'That splendid big sword!' went on Grandad, remembering. 'Just right for me, William! Look, if ever I've lived before, that old sword once belonged to me! I feel it! That's one thing I won't sell, mind! I'll keep it just for the sake of swinging it round my head, when I lose my temper!'

'Yes, yes – but I hope you'll be sure to stand in the middle of an empty room if you do that,' said Mr Finniston, a little alarmed at the fierce look in the old man's eye. 'You won't be allowed to keep all the gold, I'm afraid – there's such a thing as treasure trove, you know – some finds go to the Crown, and I fear that will be one of them. And the jewellery too perhaps. But you'll get the value back; and the suits of armour and the swords – you'll be able to make a mint of money on those!'

'Enough for *two* new tractors?' said Great-Grandad. 'Enough for a new Land Rover? That one my grandson has, it jolts every bone in my body! Look now, William – we've got to get men digging on that site – uncovering all those cellars. What say we keep on the men that fellow Henning's got? We shan't let *him* excavicate, or whatever it's called, any more. HA! That fellow gets under my skin, and sets me itching all over. Now I can scratch him out! And see here, William, you'll shut up this shop of yours and be my adviser, won't you? I won't have that American talking me down – or that fellow Durleston!'

'*You'd* better stop talking for a bit, Grandad, you're getting too red in the face,' said Mr Finniston. 'You'll go pop if you excite yourself much more! Go home now, and I'll be up tomorrow morning. I'll arrange about the workmen too. And don't you play about with that old sword too much – you might cut off somebody's head by mistake!'

'So I might, so I might,' said Great-Grandad, with a sly look in his eye. 'Now, if that Junior got in the way when I was swinging my sword . . . it's all right, William, it's all right! Just my joke, you know, just my joke!'

And chuckling deep down in his long beard, Great-Grandad strode off, turned up the little lane, and walked back to the farmhouse, feeling very pleased indeed with life!

Mr Henning, Mr Durleston and Junior did not come back that night. Apparently they were all so excited over the excavations they had made in the drilling down through the cellar roof, that they stayed too long at the hotel and decided to spend the night there, much to Mrs Philpot's relief.

'Most farm people like to go to bed about nine o'clock,' said Mr Henning, 'and it's already gone that now. We'll go over tomorrow morning and we'll get them to sign that agreement you've drawn up, Durleston. They're so short of money they'd sign anything. And mind you cry down what we think we've found, so that they won't expect any *more* than £5,000. We're going to make our fortunes over this!'

So, next morning, the two men, with an excited Junior whom Mr Durleston found most annoying, arrived at the farmhouse at about ten o'clock. They had telephoned to say they would be there then, and would bring the agreement with them, '. . . and the cheque, Mrs Philpot, the cheque!' purred Mr Henning down the phone.

When they arrived there was quite a company there to greet them! There was old Great-Grandad, his grandson Mr Philpot and his wife, the twins, of course, and old Mr Finniston, sniffing a fight, his dull eyes bright this morning for the first time in years! He sat at the back, wondering what was going to happen.

All the Five were there too, Timmy wondering what the excitement was. He kept as close to George as he could, and growled at Snippet every time the excited little poodle came near. Snippet didn't mind! He could always growl back!

A car purred up the drive, and in came Mr Henning, Mr Durleston and Junior, whose face was one big grin.

'Hallo, folks!' said Junior, in his usual jaunty manner. 'How's tricks?'

Nobody answered except Timmy, and he gave a small growl, which made Junior skip out of the way quickly. 'You shut up,' he said to Timmy.

'Did you have your breakfast in bed at the hotel, little boy?' said George suddenly. 'Do you remember the last time you had it in bed here, and Timmy pulled . . .'

'Aw shucks!' said Junior, sulkily. 'Skip it, sister!' He subsided after that, and sat down by his father. Then began a short, sharp and satisfactory meeting – from Mr Philpot's point of view!

'Er – Mr Philpot – it's my very great pleasure to say

that I have been advised by Mr Durleston to offer you a further cheque for £5,000,' said Mr Henning smoothly. 'While we are rather *disappointed* in what appears to be in the cellars of the castle, we feel it would only be fair to offer you the sum we suggested before. Is that right, Mr Durleston?'

'Absolutely,' said Mr Durleston in a business-like voice, and glared round through his horn-rimmed glasses. 'I've the agreement here. Mr Henning is being very generous. Very. The cellars are *most* disappointing.'

'I'm sorry about that,' said Mr Philpot. 'I hold a different opinion – and my adviser, Mr Finniston, upholds me in this. We are going to excavate the site ourselves, Mr Henning – and then, if any disappointment lies in wait, *we* shall be the ones to suffer, not you.'

'What's all this?' said Mr Henning, glaring round. 'Durleston, what do you say to that? Bit of double-crossing, isn't it?'

'Offer him £10,000,' said Mr Durleston, looking startled at this unexpected set-back.

'You can offer me a hundred thousand if you like, but I tell you, I prefer to do the excavation myself on my own land,' said Mr Philpot. 'What is more, I will return the cheque you gave me yesterday – and as I intend to keep on the men you engaged, I will pay them myself for their work. So do not trouble to dismiss them. They will now be working for *me.*'

'But this is MONSTROUS!' shouted Mr Henning, losing his temper, and jumping to his feet. He banged on the table, and glared at Mr and Mrs Philpot. 'What do you expect to find in those derelict old cellars? We drilled right through yesterday, and there's practically *nothing* there! I made you a very generous offer. I'll raise it to £10,000!'

'No,' said Mr Philpot, quietly. But Great-Grandad had had enough of Mr Henning's shouting and raging. He stood up too, and bellowed so loudly that everyone jumped, and Timmy began to bark. Snippet at once fled to the kitchen cupboard and hid there.

'HA! NOW YOU LISTEN TO ME!' bellowed Great-Grandad. 'This farm belongs to ME, and my GRAND-SON, and it'll go to my GREAT GRANDSON, sitting yonder. A finer farm there never was, and my family's had it for hundreds of years – and sad it's been for me to see it go downhill for lack of money! But now I see money, much money – down in those cellars! HA! All the money we want for tractors and bailers and com-bines and the Lord knows what! We don't want *your* money. No, SIR! You keep your dollars, you keep them. Offer me a *hundred* thousand if you like, and see what I'll say!'

Mr Henning turned swiftly and looked at Mr Durleston, who at once nodded. 'Right!' said the American to Great-Grandad. 'A hundred thousand! Done?'

'NO!' bawled Great-Grandad, enjoying himself more than he had done for years. 'There's *gold* down in those cellars – jewels – suits of armour – swords, daggers, knives – all of them centuries old . . . and . . .'

'Don't hand *me* stories like that,' said Mr Henning, sneeringly. 'You old liar!'

Great-Grandad banged his clenched fist down on the table and made everyone almost fall off their chairs. 'TWINS!' he roared. 'Fetch those things you got yesterday – go on, fetch them here. I'll show this American I'm no liar!'

And then, before the astounded eyes of Mr Henning and Mr Durleston, and of Junior, too, the twins laid the gold coins, the jewellery, and the swords and knives on the table. Mr Durleston stared as if he couldn't believe his eyes.

'Well – what do you say to *that*?' demanded Great-Grandad, banging on the table again.

Mr Durleston sat back and said one word. 'Junk!'

Then it was old Mr Finniston's turn to stand up and say a few words! Mr Durleston, who hadn't noticed the quiet old man sitting at the back, was horrified to see him there. He knew he was learned and knowledgeable, for he himself had tried to pick his brains about the old castle site.

'Ladies and gentlemen,' said Mr Finniston, just as if he were addressing a well-conducted meeting, 'I regret to say that, speaking as well-known antiquarian, I do not consider that Mr Durleston knows what he is talking about if he calls these articles junk! The things on the table are worth a small fortune to any genuine collector. I could myself sell them in London tomorrow, for far more than any sum Mr Durleston has advised Mr Henning to offer. Thank you, ladies and gentlemen!'

And he sat down, bowing courteously to the assembled company. Anne felt as if she wanted to clap him!

'Well, I don't think there's any more to say,' said Mr Philpot, getting up. 'If you'll tell me what hotel you'll be staying at, Mr Henning, I'll have your things sent there. You will certainly not wish to stay here any longer!'

'Pop, I don't *wanna* go, I wanna stay here!' howled Junior, most surprisingly. 'I wanna see the cellars exca-exculpated! I wanna dig down! I wanna STAY!'

'Well, we don't *want* you!' said Harry, fiercely. 'You and your peeping and prying and listening and boasting and tale-bearing. Cissy-boy! Breakfast in bed! Can't clean his shoes! Howls when he can't get his own way! Screams when . . .'

'That's enough, Harry,' said his mother sternly, looking quite shocked. 'I don't mind Junior staying on if he'll behave himself. It's not his fault that all this has happened.'

'I wanna *stay*!' wept Junior, and kicked out peevishly under the table. He unfortunately caught Timmy on the nose, and the dog rose in anger, growling and showing his teeth. Junior fled for his life.

'Do you *wanna* stay now?' shouted George, as he went, and the answer came back at once.

'NO!'

'Well, thanks, Timmy, for helping him to make up his mind,' said George, and patted the big dog.

Mr Henning looked as if he were about to burst. 'If that dog bites my boy, I'll have him put to sleep,' he said. 'I'll sue you, I'll . . .'

'Please go,' said Mrs Philpot, suddenly looking tired out. 'I have a lot of baking to do.'

'I shall take my time,' said Mr Henning, pompously. 'I will *not* be turned out suddenly, as if I hadn't paid my bills.'

'Seen this sword, Henning?' said old Great-Grandad, suddenly, and snatched from the table the big sword that he so much liked. 'Beauty, isn't it? The men of old knew how to deal with their enemies, didn't they? They swung at them like this – and like THAT – and . . .'

'Here, stop! You're dangerous! That sword nearly cut me!' cried Mr Henning, in a sudden panic. 'WILL you put it down?'

'No. It's mine. I'm not selling this,' said Great-Grandad, swinging the sword again. It hit the light-bulb above his head, and the glass fell with a clatter. Mr Durleston deserted Mr Henning and fled out of the kitchen at top speed, colliding violently with Bill, who was just coming in.

'Look out – he's mad – that old man's mad!' shouted Mr Durleston. 'Henning, come along before he cuts off your head!'

Mr Henning fled too. Great-Grandad pursued him to the door, breathing blood and thunder, and the two dogs barked in delight. Everyone began to laugh helplessly.

'Grandad – what's got into you?' said Mr Philpot, as the old fellow swung the sword again, his eyes bright, a broad grin on his wrinkled old face.

'Nothing! I just thought that only this sword would get rid of those fellows. Do you know what *I* call them? JUNK! Ha – wish I'd thought of that when they were here! JUNK! William Finniston, did you hear that?'

'Now you put that sword down before you damage it,' said Mr Finniston, who knew how to manage Great-Grandad, 'and you and I will go down to the old inn and talk over what we're going to do about all this treasure trove. You just put that sword down first – NO, Grandad, I am NOT going to take you into the inn carrying that sword!'

Mrs Philpot heaved a sigh of relief when the two old fellows went off down the lane, leaving the sword safely behind. She sat down, and, to the children's horror, began to cry!

'Now, now – don't take any notice of me!' she said, when the twins ran to her in dismay. 'I'm crying for joy – to have got rid of them – and to know I've not got to pinch and scrape any more – or to take in visitors. To think that your dad can buy the farm machinery he wants – and . . . oh dear, what a baby I am, acting like this!'

'I say, Mrs Philpot – would you like *us* to leave too?' asked Anne, suddenly realising that she and the others were ranked as 'visitors', and must have been an added burden for poor Mrs Philpot.

'Oh no, my dear, no – you're not really visitors, you're *friends*!' said Mrs Philpot, smiling through her tears. 'And what's more I shan't charge your mothers a single penny for having you here – see what good fortune you've brought us!'

'All right – we'll stay. We'd love to,' said Anne. 'We wouldn't miss seeing what else is down in those castle cellars for anything. Would we, George?'

'Gosh, no!' said George. 'We want to be in on everything. This is just about the most exciting adventure we've ever had!'

'We always say that!' said Anne. 'But the nice part about this one is – it isn't finished yet! We'll be able to go and watch the workmen and their drills. We'll be able to help in moving all the exciting old things out of their hiding places – we'll hear what prices you get for them – and see the new tractor! Honestly, I really do believe the *second* part of this adventure will be better than the first! Don't you think so, Timmy?'

'woof'! said Timmy, and wagged his tail so hard that he knocked Snippet right over.

Well, goodbye, Five! Enjoy the rest of your adventures, and have a good time – and DO make sure that Grandad is careful with that great old sword!

A complete list of the FAMOUS FIVE ADVENTURES *by Enid Blyton*

A complete list of the SECRET SEVEN ADVENTURES _by Enid Blyton_